FORTUNE'S MAGIC FARM

FORTUNE'S MAGIC FARM

BY SUZANNE SELFORS

Illustrated by Catia Chien

Little, Brown and Company
New York   Boston

Also by Suzanne Selfors:

To Catch a Mermaid
Smells Like Dog
Smells Like Treasure

Copyright © 2009 by Suzanne Selfors
Illustrations copyright © 2009 by Catia Chien

Little, Brown and Company

Hachette Book Group
237 Park Avenue, New York, NY 10017
Visit our website at www.lb-kids.com

Little, Brown and Company is a division of Hachette Book Group, Inc.
The Little, Brown name and logo are trademarks of Hachette Book Group, Inc.

The publisher is not responsible for websites (or their content) that are not owned by the publisher.

First Paperback Edition: February 2012
Originally published in hardcover in March 2009 by Little, Brown and Company

Library of Congress Cataloging-in-Publication Data

Selfors, Suzanne.
Fortune's magic farm / by Suzanne Selfors ; illustrated by Catia Chien.—1st ed.
p. cm.
Summary: Rescued from a rainy, boggy town where she works in a dismal factory, ten-year-old orphan Isabelle learns that she is the last surviving member of a family that tends the world's only remaining magic-producing farm.
ISBN 978-0-316-01818-0 (hc) / ISBN 978-0-316-01819-7 (pb)
[1. Orphans—Fiction. 2. Magic—Fiction. 3. Farms—Fiction.] I. Chien, Catia, ill. II. Title.
PZ7.S456922Fo 2009
[Fic]—dc22

2008012493

10 9 8 7 6 5 4 3

RRD-C

Book design by Maria Mercado

Printed in the United States of America

For my Isabelle—

seed collector, bug inspector, creature protector.

Acknowledgments

As usual, my deepest gratitude to my hand-holding, confidence-boosting, never-tiring writing group members: Anjali Banerjee, Carol Cassella, Sheila Rabe, Elsa Watson, and Susan Wiggs. How I would manage without them is beyond me.

Once again, heartfelt thanks to my editor, Jennifer Hunt; her assistant, T. S. Ferguson; and my literary agent, Michael Bourret, for their continued enthusiasm for my work. They do all the mysterious "business" stuff that I am happy to avoid.

And finally, thanks to you for venturing into this story about Isabelle and her magical journey. I loved every minute of writing and I hope you find her journey as fun and as satisfying as I did.

Contents

Chapter One
A SLIMY GIFT

Isabelle stood beneath a sky as gray as a pair of filthy socks. A horde of factory workers pushed past her, eager to get home to their suppers. Having eaten only half a cheese sandwich for lunch, Isabelle ached with hunger, but she needed to run an important errand before going back to the boardinghouse — a secret errand that couldn't wait.

"I can't come with you," said Gwen, who knew all about the secret errand because she was Isabelle's best friend. "I've got stupid dish duty tonight. See ya in the morning." She wiped her runny nose on her sleeve, then disappeared into the crowd.

"See ya," Isabelle called, zipping her yellow rain slicker all the way to her chin. Poor Gwen. Dish duty was never fun, though secret errands almost always were.

Clutching an empty water bottle, Isabelle hurried away from Runny Cove's Magnificently Supreme Umbrella Factory, where she had spent the entire day standing at a conveyor belt pressing labels onto boxes. Not the way most ten-year-olds would choose to spend the day, but Isabelle had no choice. Even though the work left her fingertips raw and made the soles of her feet ache, she never complained. Her boring job was the only reason she could buy half a cheese sandwich and a rain slicker. Without the umbrella factory, Isabelle would have nothing.

She followed the gravel road that led from the factory to the village of Runny Cove. Raindrops drummed against the sides of her plastic hood, a sound so commonplace that she barely even noticed. It rained every day in Runny Cove. It had for as long as Isabelle could remember. Sometimes the drops were as fat as thumbprints; sometimes they were almost invisible, forming a veil of mist. Sometimes they beat down so hard that they stung Isabelle's skin, while other times they dropped lazily from the sky like parachutists.

Because the clouds never parted in Runny Cove, the village was perpetually cast in a depressing shade of sludge — the same color as the gunky stuff that clogs up bathroom sinks. Never had Isabelle basked in the sun's warmth or strolled in the moon's light. Never had she known what it felt like to be completely dry. That was the cruel reality of Runny Cove and that is why no one ever moved there. Isabelle couldn't blame them. Who would want to live in a gloomy place by the sea where it never stops raining, and where everyone's skin is puckered and pale and covered in mold?

While most of the villagers chose to sit around and complain about the mud, acting all dreary about the rain as if it had seeped inside their skin and had drowned their spirits, Isabelle's spirit refused to be extinguished, no matter how waterlogged it got. Ever heard the saying that if you've got lemons, you should make lemonade? Well, when you've got mud you might as well make mud pies, or mud forts, or mud slides. And that's exactly what Isabelle and her friends did. A lowly substance, mud, but with the right outlook it can offer up endless possibilities.

While the rest of the workers headed into the village, Isabelle took a sharp turn off the road and started across the sand dunes. Dusk was falling, but like everyone else in Runny Cove, she was accustomed to dim light. Up and over the dunes she went, her mind fixated on her secret errand. She needed to get it done quickly so she could get back to Mama Lu's Boardinghouse for supper.

Up and over, over and up she hurried, slowing only to cough. People who spend their days in damp undershirts and wet socks tend to get colds, which is the reason why most everyone in Runny Cove had a runny nose and a rib-splitting cough.

Though the crisp evening air tickled Isabelle's congested lungs, she kept her pace until she reached the driftwood forest. The logs lay in chaotic piles, some with sharp jutting branches, others with rotten patches that could break a leg. Isabelle had never seen a tightrope walker but she resembled one as she held out her arms and tiptoed across, still clutching the empty bottle. She didn't feel a bit scared, since she had ventured to the beach many times by herself to explore or collect treasures. Excitement drove her onward. Her errand meant doing something different, something interesting, and she was one of those people who always managed to find bits of *interesting* in places where other people never looked.

As she crossed the driftwood, she sang one of her little songs at just the right tempo to match her careful steps. She sang loudly because there was no one around to yell, "Hey kid! Stop making all that racket. Yer giving me a headache!" Here's what she sang.

The Nowhere Song

**Beyond the town, beyond the mill
beyond the river, beyond the hill
lies the land of Nowhere
and Nowhere lies there still,
for no one goes to Nowhere
and no one ever will.**

It was a song she had made up about the mysterious place of her birth. At least that's what her Grandma Maxine had always told her whenever she had asked, "Where did I come from?"

"Nowhere."

"Is it far away?"

"I don't know. No one knows."

As much as Isabelle loved her grandmother, the lack of information drove her crazy. A person has the right to know where she comes from. It's a perfectly reasonable request, not like asking for a new rain slicker when the old one only has a couple of holes. Gwen knew about her parents. She knew that her mother had died giving birth to her and that her father had died from a fever. It didn't make being an orphan any easier but at least Gwen knew. Isabelle knew nothing.

"You've got to know something, Grandma. Think harder and you'll remember."

"It's no use asking me so many questions, Isabelle. All I know is that I found you one stormy morning. Nothing else. Just you, lying on the doorstep without a stitch of clothing, screaming so loud you drowned out the wind and rain. It seemed like you just appeared out of thin air."

"But I must have come from somewhere."

"As far as I can tell you came from nowhere, so please stop asking."

A girl who begins her life on a doorstep, without a note or clue of any kind, has a choice. She can believe that she was abandoned because no one wanted her, and she can feel like the most unimportant person in the world. Or she can believe, as Isabelle did, that because her origins were shrouded in mystery, that she must be an *extra* important person. A special person. A person like no other person.

For a secret birth is like a secret errand — sure to yield something *interesting*.

Isabelle reached the edge of the driftwood forest and, with a graceful jump, landed in the hard, wet sand that lay at the water's edge. The cove formed a crescent as gray as the sky above, littered with the hulls of long-abandoned fishing boats. Creosote-covered pilings poked out of the water, all that remained of the docks that used to line the beach.

Grandma Maxine had told her that the boats used to go out each morning and return each evening, overflowing with fish. But no one fished the cove anymore, not since the fish had gone away.

Isabelle twisted the cap off the empty bottle and waded into the water. As she submerged the bottle, air bubbles rose to the surface, bobbing between raindrops. When the bottle had filled, she recapped it and shoved it into her pocket. Her stomach growled. Mama Lu would be serving supper soon.

Her errand completed, Isabelle was about to start home when a roar rose above the rain's drumming — a roar far too loud to be her stomach.

Something moved in the water where the cove met the sea. Isabelle pushed off her hood, trying to get a better view. The something was much bigger than she, and swimming toward her. She took a few steps backward as it moved closer. She'd never seen anything like it. Could it be dangerous?

She ran up the beach to the edge of the driftwood forest, where she watched, open-mouthed, as the large thing emerged from the shallow water. It was a creature of some sort, and it pulled its enormous, blubbery body onto the sand with a pair of front flippers. The strangest nose hung from the middle of its face, swaying back and forth as it heaved itself up the beach. She couldn't see its mouth but imagined a vast row of sharp teeth. If it didn't eat her alive, surely it would flatten her like a skipping stone. Terrified, she scrambled up some driftwood but lost her footing and fell back onto the sand.

ROARRRRR!

With a burst of speed, the creature galloped up the beach and parked itself at Isabelle's feet. She froze, remembering that the fishermen who had fished the cove long ago had believed in sea monsters that sank ships and ate the crew.

Hot breath seared Isabelle's face. Large black eyes, surrounded by folds of skin, stared down at her. "Please don't eat me," she begged, squeezing her eyes shut. Being eaten alive wasn't something she wanted to watch. She waited for deep, horrible pain. But a few moments passed and nothing happened. Slowly, she opened her eyes.

Still staring, the monster cocked its head. Raindrops rolled down skin that looked like rubber. It sniffed her hair with its long nose.

"Please, please don't eat me," Isabelle whimpered, scooting back against the driftwood pile.

It raised its nose and opened its mouth. Isabelle squealed and pushed against the wood, hoping to find a spot where she could disappear. But she was trapped. She was going to die without having said goodbye to her grandmother or to Gwen. She was about to become supper! "Help!" she cried, though she knew no one would hear.

The sea monster took a great breath, then sneezed. The force of the sneeze knocked Isabelle sideways. Slime shot out the end of the dangly nose and landed in Isabelle's short hair. Disgusting! "Cover your nose when you sneeze," Grandma Maxine always said. But Isabelle wasn't about to correct a sea monster's manners.

"You can sneeze on me as much as you'd like. Just please don't eat me." She pulled on her hood as the creature took another breath and sneezed again. This time, something else flew out of its nose and landed with a *thunk* in Isabelle's lap.

The creature tapped its flipper impatiently and grunted, as if waiting for something. The rain beat harder. Isabelle peered out from under her hood. She didn't know what to do. What could it possibly be waiting for?

"Bless you?" she whispered.

It continued to stare.

"Bless you two times?"

The nose reached forward and pointed at Isabelle's lap. She grimaced, expecting to find a giant booger, but found, instead, a slime-covered red apple.

A real, honest-to-goodness apple.

No apples grew in Runny Cove or in the wetlands that lay outside the village. Apples occasionally showed up at the factory's grocery store, but only Mr. Supreme's assistants could afford to buy them. Isabelle had never tasted one. She had never even held one. She picked it up. It would cost an entire day's wages to buy one half the size. The sea monster grunted again. "Oh, I'm sorry. Here." She held it out. Should she stick the apple back up its nose?

To her amazement, the sea monster shook its head.

"Don't you want it back?"

It shook its head again. Then, with a roar that vibrated Isabelle's teeth, it turned and made its way back to the water. It hadn't eaten her. It hadn't flattened her. It had only sneezed on her. "THANK YOU!" she yelled, waving the apple.

It turned and nodded, its nose bouncing up and down. Then, it swam out of sight.

"Wow," Isabelle whispered.

Other than being left on a doorstep, that was the most special thing that had ever happened to Isabelle. Even though slime coated her hair and face, and even though she had been scared half to death, she smiled. Gwen would never believe it. Wouldn't Grandma Maxine be surprised? No one in Runny Cove had ever met a sea monster. No factory worker had ever been given an apple.

She checked to make certain that the water bottle was safe in one pocket and tucked the apple securely into another pocket. Then she climbed onto the driftwood pile and ran back toward the village, feeling extra, extra special.

Chapter Two
MAMA LU

Water sloshed against Isabelle's boots as she ran down Boggy Lane. The cobblestone lane dipped into the lowest part of the village, so it was always flooded. As her hood bounced at the back of her neck, rain washed all the sea monster snot from her face and hair.

Old, battered boardinghouses lined Boggy Lane. Lights glowed from kitchen windows. Greasy odors wafted through cracks in the house boards, aggravating Isabelle's hunger pains. She wondered if the apple would be edible after traveling inside a nose. She plucked it from her pocket and held it beneath a gushing rainspout. Bigger and shinier than any apple in the factory store, she could have eaten it right there, but then she'd have no proof of her adventure. Besides, something that wonderful had to be shared.

Boggy Lane took a sharp turn, then ended at Mama Lu's Boardinghouse. A vacancy sign swayed in the window, pushed by the wind and rain. No one had moved to Runny Cove for as long as Isabelle could remember, but Mama Lu still insisted on advertising. Isabelle ran up the stone steps and threw herself against the front door, which swelled in particularly nasty weather and needed a good shove to open.

"Yer late!" Mama Lu hollered from the kitchen.

"Sorry," Isabelle called, closing the door. Of course, she didn't regret her trip to the beach, not one bit.

The entryway felt chilly, as usual. The sour smell of boiled cabbage hung in the air. A frying pan sat on the floor, collecting water that dripped from a seam in the wall. Isabelle slipped off her boots and placed them neatly at the end of the boot shelf. She removed her rain slicker and hung it on the rack next to the other slickers. She decided to leave the filled water bottle in her slicker's pocket and get it after supper. The apple, however, was another matter. Mama Lu liked to snoop through pockets and while she'd have no interest in a bottle filled with seawater, if she found the apple she'd claim it for herself.

"This house belongs to me," she often reminded her tenants. "So everything in it belongs to me, too."

Isabelle tucked the apple into the waistband of her canvas pants. Her flannel shirt, a hand-me-down from another tenant, was four sizes too large, so it did a good job concealing the lump.

"Did ya check fer slugs?" Mama Lu bellowed. The boardinghouse's proprietor despised slugs. In fact, she hated them so much that the mere act of seeing one drove her into a tizzy. Unfortunately, Runny Cove possessed more slugs than any other place on earth. The little gastropods bred in every damp nook and cranny the village had to offer. They gobbled up anything the villagers tried to grow, leaving trails of slime in their wake. If a slug wanted to move across town, it would attach itself to a boot or pant leg when a villager walked down the street, or drop from an eave to hitchhike on a hood or in someone's hair. Mama Lu had decreed that anyone who brought a slug into her house would lose blanket privileges for a month. "Did ya check?"

In all her excitement, Isabelle had forgotten to check. "Yes, I checked," she lied, quickly sliding her hands through her hair.

"I hate those slimy things," Mama Lu complained from the kitchen. "I hate their quivery antennas and their squishy bodies."

Isabelle entered the kitchen, where six tenants sat around a warped table, coughing and wheezing, sharing the same cold. Even though only two of the tenants were related by blood, everyone looked alike. In fact, most of Runny Cove's villagers shared a similar appearance. Their skin, having never been exposed to the sun, was translucent, and their eyes were light blue. And every hair on every head was gray, even ten-year-old Isabelle's hair. Some said that the dreary sky had fallen into their hair, but Isabelle's grandmother said that everyone's hair was gray because gray is the color of sadness.

In the boardinghouse, only Mama Lu looked different. She dyed her hair with an expensive paste that turned it as black as a beach rock. She had spending money, a luxury none of her tenants had. In exchange for most of their factory pay, the tenants got an uncomfortable twin bed, a cold breakfast, and a lukewarm supper.

Isabelle reached for a tray. "Sit down," Mama Lu ordered. "Ya can feed yer precious granny when yer done."

Isabelle squeezed in between Bert and Boris, the elderly

toothless twins who lived in the basement. "Hello, Isabelle," Bert whispered.

"Hello, Isabelle," Boris whispered.

"Hello." She liked to sit between the twins because they didn't smell too bad, not like Mr. Limewig, who thought that with all the rain, he didn't need to shower. The other tenants nodded, then, between coughs, slurped their soup. Mama Lu plunked Isabelle's bowl and soupspoon onto the table.

"Yer a rude one, being so late," Mama Lu said. "I've got better things to do than wait around fer you."

"Sorry," Isabelle said, knowing Mama Lu had nothing better to do.

"Sorry," Mama Lu repeated in a whiny voice. "Sorry don't mean nothing to my swollen feet." She pointed to her feet, which were crammed into pink fuzzy slippers. Swollen or not, they sure looked enormous.

Isabelle dipped the wooden spoon into her bowl and sipped. The thin broth, a tasteless brew made from cabbage and carrots, was still a bit warm and it felt good going down. Isabelle would have voluntarily worked dish duty for just a dash of salt, but Mama Lu would let no one touch her salt. She considered salt to be a sacred weapon in her one-woman battle against the slugs of Runny Cove. She always carried a canister in her bathrobe pocket and would pull it out quick-draw style upon spotting a slug. It wasn't a pretty sight when a slug got salted because the salt sucked all the moisture from the slug's plump little body, leaving a puddle of goo. Isabelle hated it when Mama Lu salted slugs.

But that evening, Isabelle wasn't thinking about slugs. *I found an apple, I found an apple, I found an apple,* she sang in her head.

Mama Lu tossed a basket of rock-hard biscuits onto the table, then went to powder her nose. Isabelle pulled the basket close, took one of the biscuits, and quickly warmed it between her palms. No one understood why, but Isabelle's hands had always been warmer than everyone else's hands. She never needed mittens, a luxury that few could afford. In winter, when the rain turned to hail and the front doorknob froze, she simply gripped the knob until it thawed. When her grandmother's arthritic knee acted up, she wrapped her hands around the knee until the muscle relaxed. But biscuit-warming could only be done in Mama Lu's absence, so Isabelle hurriedly warmed another and another, passing them down the table.

Mama Lu returned, her nose all powdery, and climbed onto her *observation chair* — a tall chair with ladders on each side that sat at the head of the kitchen table. The mysterious words LIFEGUARD ON DUTY had been painted on the back a long time ago. The chair creaked as Mama Lu heaved her large thighs up each rung, pausing halfway to catch her breath. At the top, she adjusted her blue bathrobe, then sat down with a loud "hmphhh."

From her perch, Mama Lu kept an eye on her tenants in case one of them tried to steal something. Bert had told Isabelle that sitting higher than everyone else made Mama Lu feel important. Being the only person in Runny Cove found on a doorstep made Isabelle feel important.

"Which one of ya stupid dunderheads is going to bring me my cheese?" Mama Lu asked, her two chins jiggling. "Get a move on. I'm starvin' to death."

Isabelle hoped it wasn't her turn, because if she had to climb that ladder, the apple might slip out from under her waistband. But to her relief, Mrs. Wormbottom climbed the ladder and handed up a platter that held slices of yellow and white cheese, some with holes, some with crusty rinds, and some with specks of blue mold. As Mrs. Wormbottom returned to her bland soup, Mama Lu began feasting.

"Moos gmph sumpin interumbling to smph?" Mama Lu asked with a mouth full of cheese. Even though they couldn't understand the words, everyone at the table knew the question because every night Mama Lu asked, "Who's got something interesting to say?" It was a dreaded question. Having something interesting to say was as rare in Runny Cove as an apple. For most of the tenants, each day yielded the exact same events so the days blended together, forming one gigantic blob of *un*interesting. Since Isabelle often managed to find bits of interesting, it usually fell upon her shoulders to answer the dreaded question.

But on this night she held her tongue. No way was she going to tell Mama Lu about the apple.

"Rain came down extra hard today," Mr. Wormbottom said. "Sprang a leak in my window."

Mama Lu scowled and pointed a floppy slice of white

17

cheese at him. "Ya wouldn't be complaining about yer accommodations, would ya?"

Mrs. Wormbottom gulped. "No, he's not complaining. Not complaining one bit."

"I'm just making conversation," Mr. Wormbottom said. "*Interesting* conversation."

"Pathetic conversation, that's what yer making. I don't want to hear no more about the rain. In fact, anyone who talks about the rain ever again will lose spoon privileges," she snarled. "One of ya morons better come up with something interesting."

All eyes turned toward Isabelle.

She sank low on the bench, burying her nose in her soup bowl. No way.

"Don't anyone got anything to say? Yer the boringest tenants in the whole world. Bunch of dimwits, the whole lot of ya."

"Got a rock stuck in the heel of my boot on the way home," Mr. Limewig said, widening his eyes hopefully.

"Rock?" Mama Lu cried. "What's interesting about a rock?"

"Found a mushroom growing under my bed," Mrs. Limewig said.

Like slugs, mushrooms cropped up all over Runny Cove — along the road, in ditches, under kitchen sinks. But only Isabelle grew them between her toes and no one knew why. And while most everyone in Runny Cove had to deal with itchy mold patches, Isabelle grew more mold patches than anyone else. She had a tendency to grow lichen on her scalp, as well.

"Mushroom? There's nothing interesting about a mushroom." Mama Lu's face turned red. "What about you?" She pointed at Isabelle. "Ya always got something to say. Ya think yer so special just because ya got found on a doorstep and the rest of us didn't." She shoved two cubes of orange cheese into her mouth. "My yus ya mate?"

Isabelle tried to disappear behind Bert's damp sleeve.

Mama Lu swallowed. "I said, why was ya late? Was ya playing in the mud again? Making stupid muddy things? Was ya poking around like yer always doing, looking here, looking there? Huh? Where was ya?"

The tenants stopped slurping. Only drumming rain and congested breathing could be heard. Isabelle strained to find a good answer. Say the wrong thing and Mama Lu could withhold tea or toilet paper privileges, or put Isabelle on all-night slug patrol. "I went to the beach," Isabelle replied.

"What?" Mama Lu leaned forward. The chair creaked and swayed. "What did ya say?" Boris gently patted Isabelle's arm, encouraging her to continue.

"I said I went to the beach. The beach is very interesting. Did you know that there are bugs that hop in the sand?"

Mama Lu scowled. "Why would anyone go to the beach? Only a brainless half-wit would go to the beach. There's nothing at the beach." She raised her bushy eyebrows. "Did ya find something at the beach?"

Isabelle shook her head. "No. Not a thing. Nothing at all. Just bugs in the sand."

"Them bugs better stay in the sand. I don't want no bugs in this house." Mama Lu picked a bit of cheese rind from her teeth, then slammed her fist on the armrest. "Is it too much to ask fer a little conversation? I slave away all day fer the lot of ya and all I ask is fer a little bit of interesting conversation."

Isabelle couldn't imagine Mama Lu slaving away. In fact, she had never seen her do any work besides throwing cabbage into a pot and boiling it.

"I demand that ya tell me something interesting. Something I've never heard before. If ya don't, then there'll be no food fer yer precious granny tonight."

Once again, all eyes turned Isabelle's way. Her grandmother couldn't go without food because she was sick and weak. Isabelle would have to reveal her secret. She placed her hands over the lump in her shirt. "I . . . I . . ."

Just then, the front door burst open.

Chapter Three

STRANGE DELIVERIES

Gertrude Bolt, owner of Gertrude's Boardinghouse, stumbled into the kitchen, waving her hands as if they were on fire. She hadn't bothered to put on a slicker, so her green bathrobe sparkled with droplets. "Mama Lu, Mama Lu," she shrieked. "Wait 'til you hear, wait 'til you hear."

Relieved, Isabelle released a big breath. Hopefully, Gertrude's interruption would save her from having to reveal her secret.

The observation chair creaked as Mama Lu leaned over its armrest. "Did ya check fer slugs? I ain't listening 'til ya check fer slugs."

Gertrude shook her bathrobe. "No slugs."

"Then what is it, Gertie?" Mama Lu wrung her hands excitedly. "It must be something good to get ya out at this late hour. Is it something good?"

"They're thieves. That's what they are. Thieves."

"Thieves?" Mama Lú smiled, her upper lip stretching across her crooked teeth. She and Gertrude had built a friendship around the fact that they loved to say bad things about other people. "Now *that* sounds interesting."

It does sound interesting, Isabelle thought.

"I'm coming right down." The tenants averted their eyes as Mama Lu began her descent. No one wanted to see her enormous striped bloomers. When she reached the floor, the chair sighed with relief. "So, Gertie? Who is these thieves?"

Gertrude frowned at the sickly tenants. "Do we have to talk in front of them? Let's sit in your parlor."

Mama Lu led Gertrude into the parlor, where a weak fire burned. The damp peat sputtered and sizzled. She and Gertrude sat on the only couch while the tenants tried their best to stifle their coughs so they could eavesdrop. Fortunately, both of the landladies spoke in obnoxiously loud voices.

Gertrude cleared her throat. "You know my young tenant, that rotten little girl named Gwen?"

Isabelle sat up straight, pursing her lips angrily. How dare she call Gwen, her best friend, rotten? A person could call Gwen sad, on account of her being an orphan, and could even call her gloomy, on account of her having to work in a factory. But rotten was totally unfair.

"Yes, I know the one. Always has that snotty nose. What has she done? Has she done something wicked?"

"She brought home an apple," Gertrude said. "A red apple."

Isabelle nearly knocked her soup bowl over. She wrapped her arms around her precious lump. How could this be?

"An apple?" Mama Lu asked. "How could she afford such a thing?"

"She said it fell from the sky."

"Say what?"

Gertrude raised her voice. "She said it fell from the sky. Said a black bird dropped it on her head. I think she's lying. That's what I think."

Mama Lu snorted. "'Course she's lying. A bird can't carry

no apple. She stole it. No doubt about it. Where's the apple now?"

"I took it," Gertrude said proudly. "Put it in my icebox. If it's stolen property, the authorities should be told." The authorities boiled down to one person — Mr. Earl Hench, the umbrella factory's security guard and Gertrude's boyfriend.

Boris leaned close to Isabelle. "Do you think Gwen stole the apple?" he asked quietly.

Isabelle shook her head. "No way." If a sea monster could carry an apple, then so could a bird. But how strange that after a lifetime without apples, she and Gwen had each gotten one on the same day.

The tenants tilted their heads as the parlor conversation continued.

"She's a thief. They're all thieves. Why do ya think I sit in that chair?" Mama Lu asked Gertrude. "So I can keep an eye on my tenants. Which reminds me . . ." She stomped back into the kitchen and quickly counted the soupspoons. "Don't think fer one minute that just because I'm in the parlor ya numb-headed fools can steal from me."

The tenants, whose heads *were* slightly numb from the cold, but who *weren't* thieves or fools, didn't defend themselves. It would only result in double dishwashing duty or loss of towel privileges. They put up with the abuse because they couldn't afford to go anywhere else.

"Mama Lu," Gertrude called from the couch. "There's more, I tell you. Much more."

"More?" Mama Lu waddled back to the parlor. "Do tell, Gertie."

"Do you know that boy who lives with his father on Dripping Alley? The ugly boy with the birthmark on his cheek? He came home with an apple too. I know because my *boyfriend*, Earl Hench, saw him carrying it and confiscated it on account of it was stolen."

Isabelle couldn't believe what she was hearing. Leonard was the only boy in Runny Cove with a birthmark on his cheek. He sat at lunch break with Gwen and Isabelle. Being the only ten-year-olds in the factory, they tended to stick together. "He said that he was walking home when he saw an orange cat sleeping in the alley. When he tried to catch the cat it ran off but guess what it had been sleeping on?"

The tenants looked at one another and silently mouthed, *an apple.*

"Well? Can you guess?" Gertrude asked.

"Course I can guess. I'm not stupid." Mama Lu cleared her throat. "But . . . but ya go ahead and tell me anyway."

"He told Earl Hench, my *boyfriend*, that the cat had been sleeping on the apple. I think it's another lie."

"'Course it's a lie. There ain't no cats in Runny Cove, haven't been since I was a girl."

"She's right," Mr. Wormbottom whispered. "No cats since I was a boy."

Isabelle had never seen a cat, but she knew what they looked like because her grandmother had described them. Three apples to three friends on the same day. Nothing this exciting had happened in Runny Cove since Mr. Philbert had gotten lost in the fog. Talk about *interesting*.

"I think they're conspiring," Gertrude stated. "Starting up a ring of thieves, that's what I think. First it's apples, then it's our jewelry, then it's your cheese."

"My cheese?"

Isabelle wanted to shout out, *You're wrong!* But such a statement would result in some kind of terrible punishment. Who cared what Gertrude Bolt and Mama Lu thought, anyway? Isabelle knew that her friends weren't thieves. She could hardly wait to see them at the factory tomorrow so they could share their stories. How slowly the night would pass.

Gertrude had more to say. "But when my *boyfriend*, Earl Hench, tried to take a bite of the apple, it turned all black and powdery like fireplace ashes. But the one I took from Gwen is good, all shiny and red."

"You know, Gertie," Mama Lu said greedily, "why don't ya go and get it and we'll bake it here. Nothing better than a baked apple, all golden and juicy."

Isabelle clenched her fists. That wasn't fair. Gwen should get to eat the apple. The landladies had more food than they needed. She'd definitely save some of her apple for her friends and give it to them at the factory tomorrow.

"Finish yer dinners!" Mama Lu hollered, sticking her dyed head back into the kitchen. No tenant was allowed to linger at the table after dinner or mingle in the parlor, so they wandered off to their rooms.

Isabelle was eager to get upstairs. She took a tray from

the counter, then ladled the last bit of soup into a bowl and placed it onto the tray. She grabbed the last roll and spoon and placed them onto the tray as well. The front door creaked open. "Hurry back with yer apple," Mama Lu called. The front door closed. Isabelle moved quickly, filling a jug with tap water. After making certain that the apple was secure under her waistband, she picked up the tray and headed toward the stairs, but found Mama Lu blocking her path.

"Stop right there, Miss I'm So Special. What do ya know about them apples?" Her breath was as sharp as her cheddar dinner.

A cough tickled Isabelle's chest but she held it back. One cough and the apple might drop. Holding the tray over her hidden treasure, she smiled sweetly. "I don't know anything."

"But they're yer friends, ain't they?" Mama Lu adjusted her bathrobe's belt. "I seen ya walking with that runny-nosed girl every morning. And I seen ya talking to that ugly-faced boy. What do ya know? Ya been stealing apples too?"

"No." The apple slipped a bit. Isabelle pushed out her tummy to trap it against the waistband. But, unlike Mama Lu, Isabelle's tummy was as flat as a factory conveyor belt. The apple slipped again. If it rolled down her pant leg she'd be in big trouble. She tried to step around her landlady.

"Not so fast. What was ya doing with a bottle of dirty water in yer slicker?" Mama Lu asked, holding up Isabelle's bottle.

Isabelle couldn't tell her the real reason she had collected the seawater, the reason she had been collecting it each week for the past few months. She'd get punished if Mama Lu knew what the water was for. So she lied. "It's salty. I keep it in my room to pour on slugs if they try to get in through the window."

"Oh." Mama Lu scowled, her eyebrows knotting into a single bushy clump.

The hidden apple slipped a bit more. "Please, Mama Lu. My grandma needs her supper."

Mama Lu plunked the bottle of water onto the tray. "Yer granny had better get out of that bed soon. This ain't no hospital, ya know. She's lazy, that's what she is."

Isabelle narrowed her eyes and glared at Mama Lu. "She's sick, not lazy. And I pay the rent, don't I?" She immediately regretted her bitter tone, but Mama Lu had made her so mad she wanted to dump the seawater all over the landlady's swollen head.

"Ya'd better keep paying if ya want to keep that room."

Gertrude rushed back into the house, cradling Gwen's apple as if it were a precious infant. Mama Lu pushed Isabelle aside. As the landladies greedily smacked their lips and headed into the kitchen, Isabelle started up the stairs that led to the second floor. But halfway up she couldn't hold back the cough any longer. With the expelled breath, the apple rolled down her pant leg and landed at her feet. *Thud.* She grimaced, expecting Mama Lu to holler, "It's mine!"

Fortunately, the landladies were arguing over cooking temperature so they didn't hear the thud. What luck! Isabelle scooped up the apple and made her escape.

Chapter Four

THE ROOM ON THE
FOURTH FLOOR

Isabelle loved the fourth-floor bedroom that she shared with Grandma Maxine. Certainly the room had a few problems. The old shake roof hadn't been patched since Papa Lu's death five years ago and the walls had been built without insulation. The climb up the three flights was steep, requiring strong legs. And the climb back down to the second-floor bathroom could be treacherous, especially if Isabelle or her grandmother needed to use the bathroom during the night.

But Isabelle and her grandmother had endured all of those hardships because the uppermost room in Mama Lu's Boardinghouse came with an extra special bonus feature — for as long as Isabelle could remember, Mama Lu hadn't been able to heave herself all the way to the fourth floor. On three occasions she had almost made it. "I'm having a heart attack," she had cried, sweat pouring from her as if she had sprung leaks. "Lord have mercy, my heart can't take it." It seemed the only climbing she could manage was the ladder to her observation chair. Much to Isabelle and Grandma Maxine's delight, the fourth floor remained *Mama Lu–free.*

Isabelle hid her apple beneath a ratty napkin before she stepped onto the second-floor landing. The Wormbottoms and the twins stood in line outside the bathroom.

"Hurry up, Limewig, and do your business," Mr. Worm-bottom said, pounding on the door. "It's cold out here and you're keeping me from my bed."

"Can't rush these things," Mr. Limewig replied from behind the door.

"You want me to help you with that tray?" Bert asked.

"I can manage," Isabelle said. She wanted to share the apple with Grandma Maxine before anyone else saw it. It would be the first time she had ever been able to give her grandmother a special treat.

Boris pulled half a dinner roll from his pocket and placed it on Isabelle's tray. "Saved that for Maxine," he said with a shy smile.

"That's so sweet." Isabelle stood on tiptoe and gave him a quick kiss on his pale, wrinkled cheek. Small acts of kindness were all the tenants had. Kindness kept their hearts from turning stone cold like Mama Lu's and kept their spirits from washing down the storm drain. Isabelle vowed to save an apple slice for Boris and Bert.

Up the stairs Isabelle went. Grandma Maxine used to climb the stairs with her but over the last few months the old woman's cough had steadily worsened. First, the trek to the factory had become too difficult. Then the trek up and down the stairs. Then she hadn't been able to get out of bed. As the weeks had passed, Grandma Maxine ate less and slept longer. Isabelle had taken extra shifts at the factory to cover the lost wages and she had cared for her grandmother as best she could. She loved Grandma Maxine with her entire heart and she couldn't bear the thought that one day the old woman would die.

She just needs more time, Isabelle told herself. *Old people need more time to heal. That's all.*

Isabelle reached the fourth floor and hurried into the bedroom. Grandma Maxine lay beneath a thin, striped quilt, made from old socks. Her chest rose and fell in steady snoring. Isabelle quietly placed the tray on the bedside table. She held the apple up to the room's single bulb. The light reflected gloriously on the shiny skin. *Did it come from far away?* she wondered. *Do apples grow in Nowhere?*

"Hello, Isabelle," Grandma Maxine said, startling her.

Isabelle tucked the apple under the napkin. "Hello, Grandma. Are you feeling any better?"

"Not really. But at least it's nice and toasty in here." The bedroom didn't have a fireplace or a heater but over the last few weeks the temperature had begun to rise. "I think it's the moss carpet that's keeping it so warm."

The moss carpet was a recent addition to the room on the fourth floor. It had started with a simple clump of dark green moss that Isabelle had found on her factory locker. For some odd reason, hers was the only locker that grew moss. "Clean that locker!" Mr. Supreme's assistants always yelled. But the moss always came back. Isabelle loved the way it felt when she brushed it across her cheek, so she had carried a clump to the boardinghouse where she had placed it on her windowsill, beneath a steady drip of water. The next morning the moss had doubled in size, and after a week it had grown down the wall. In two weeks' time it had covered the entire floor. Amazingly, the moss absorbed all the nasty roof leaks yet it never felt wet.

Isabelle peeled off her damp socks and buried her aching feet in the living carpet. "It's so nice to walk on. I wish you could walk on it, Grandma."

"I wish I could too." Grandma Maxine brushed aside a vine that dangled in her face. "I think these vines are also making the room warm."

A few weeks back, Isabelle had found a tiny uprooted plant stuck to the bottom of her boot. Strange that the slugs hadn't eaten it. She had taken the plant up to her room and had tucked its roots into the moss. In a few days' time it had grown like Jack's Beanstalk, with a stem as thick as her arm and leaves that sparkled like wet sand. The vines covered the ugly plank walls, blocking all the nasty breezes.

"The vines are beautiful but they worry me," Grandma Maxine said. Her cheeks and eyes looked sunken and her skin, which was usually as translucent as Isabelle's, had taken on a grayish shade. "If Mama Lu comes up here, she'll get real mad. She'll say that you don't have permission to grow things in her house."

"Then I would tell her that I didn't grow anything," Isabelle replied. "The moss and vines grew themselves." A true and clever response. She placed the tray on her grandmother's lap. "Besides, she won't come up here. She can't get up the stairs. So please don't worry. Look, Boris saved half a roll for you."

"Such a kind man." Grandma Maxine's long gray hair had fallen loose of its braid. She raised the spoon to her mouth with a shaky hand. Isabelle's stomach clenched as she realized that her grandmother had grown even weaker. Isabelle took the spoon and started to feed her.

"I'm such a burden to you," the old woman said, tears filling her red-rimmed eyes.

"You're not a burden." It was a sweet lie. Isabelle would never say or think the word "burden," not ever, but her skinny, tired body felt differently, having worked all those extra factory hours to pay the rent.

"I don't feel very hungry." Grandma Maxine turned her head away.

"Try to eat," Isabelle insisted.

"Maybe later. Go on and feed your critters. They've been waiting all day."

"Okay."

A table, made from a discarded factory crate, sat next to Isabelle's rickety old bed. On top of the table sat a pickle jar. Mama Lu had eaten the pickles and had thrown the jar into the street. No one else seemed interested in the jar, so Isabelle had transformed it into an aquarium. The only occupant was a creature that looked like a little white rock.

"How's your barnacle?" Grandma Maxine asked.

"I think it's sleeping," Isabelle replied. She had found the lone barnacle on one of the creosote pilings. Because she had never been to school, and because Mama Lu didn't own any books on marine biology, Isabelle hadn't known what to call it. No one kept books in Runny Cove — not a single one. Paper tended to bloat and mold. Bindings disintegrated within weeks. When Mama Lu got a catalogue in the mail, the pages were always stuck together.

But Grandma Maxine knew it was called a barnacle because there had been lots of barnacles on the beach when she was little. She had studied them in school. She knew that barnacles ate tiny creatures called plankton. She knew that Isabelle would need to collect new water for the barnacle so its food supply wouldn't run out.

Isabelle opened the window and, holding the barnacle in place, carefully poured out the aquarium's old water. Rain blew against her face, soaking her short hair. *My grandmother can't hold onto a spoon anymore. Time isn't making her better.* These thoughts made Isabelle feel heavy, so she leaned against the window frame. That's when she noticed something unusual.

A tall person stood across the narrow street, on Gertrude's front porch. The porch light illuminated the edges of a long hooded cape. How strange. Most everyone in Runny Cove wore cheap plastic slickers, sold at the factory store. Who could that be? No one ever visited Runny Cove.

Grandma Maxine coughed — a deep, wet sound. Cold night air rushed through the window, so Isabelle quickly closed it. She filled the aquarium with the fresh seawater she had collected. The barnacle opened and a white feather emerged, fanning the water. "It's eating," she reported.

"That's nice," Grandma Maxine said, coughing again.

There were other critters to feed. Isabelle pulled some grass blades from her pocket and tossed them into a cracker box that she had turned into a slug garden. She dropped a small piece of rotten driftwood into an empty milk carton that she had turned into a potato bug palace.

"I'm so sleepy," Grandma Maxine murmured, closing her eyes.

"Oh, wait." Isabelle had almost forgotten. She rushed across the soft moss and grabbed the apple. "Look, I have something special for dessert."

"I'm too tired to eat."

"But it's an apple." Isabelle beamed with pride, presenting the apple with a formal bow.

Grandma Maxine opened her eyes and gasped. "An apple? Oh, Isabelle. I know we don't have enough food, but you shouldn't steal. It's wrong."

"I didn't steal it." Isabelle dug a small chunk from the apple with the spoon. "Go on, eat some." She gently pressed the piece into her grandmother's mouth.

Grandma Maxine chewed slowly, then her eyes widened. "As sweet as I remember," she said. "It's been so long."

Isabelle eagerly took a bite. Sweet juice burst onto her tongue. She wanted to shove the entire apple into her mouth. "It's the best thing ever!" She dug her grandmother another chunk. As the old woman ate, her eyes ignited, as if a lightning bolt had shot right through her. She held out her withered hand for another piece.

"How much I've missed this taste. When I was a little girl, we had an apple tree in our backyard and we ate apple pie and drank apple cider. Our neighbor had a plum tree and the church on the corner had a cherry tree. It was so different when I was little. It used to be called Sunny Cove in those days."

Isabelle knew all about her grandmother's childhood. Life in the old days sounded like a dream.

"My father loved apple cider. He was a fisherman, like all the other fathers. He'd leave in the mornings before I woke. After school I would run down to the docks and wave as his boat came in. There were plenty of fish in those days. We ate halibut and salmon and herring. My father was the best fisherman in Sunny Cove." The light faded from her eyes and she slumped against the pillow. Talking about the old days always made Grandma Maxine sad.

Isabelle knew the rest of the story. Each year the fishing fleet caught more and more fish until there were no more to catch. The people almost starved. Then the factory came and Mr. Supreme Senior gave everyone jobs. Then, mysteriously, the endless rain arrived and life changed forever. It was the saddest story she had ever heard.

The overhead light shut off with a popping sound. All the bedroom lights turned off automatically at eight o'clock. It didn't matter if Mrs. Wormbottom was darning a sock or if the twins were playing marbles. Mama Lu didn't want to spend any extra money. "Good night, Isabelle."

"Good night, Grandma."

"I love you, dearest."

"I love you too."

Then a whisper floated through the darkness. Grandma Maxine's voice was quivery and sad. "How will you take care of yourself when I'm gone?"

Isabelle removed the tray. "Don't worry about that. You need to get some sleep."

Grandma Maxine rolled over and started to snore. The sound comforted Isabelle, for a person who snores is *not gone*.

She sat on the edge of her grandmother's bed, her mind racing, thoughts turning from her grandmother's health to the day's weird events. Finding an apple beneath a cat could be simply a matter of luck. Having an apple dropped on one's head could just be a coincidence. But having a sea monster sneeze an apple onto one's lap seemed deliberate. The fact that all three apples had appeared on the same day, in a place where apples did not grow, seemed . . . miraculous! No doubt about it — Isabelle was smack dab in the middle of a mystery.

She crept to the window and leaned on the sill. That strange person in the cape had gone. The lights in Gertrude's Boardinghouse had also shut off. Gwen's window was on the back side of the house. She'd be in bed, like the others, probably crying over her lost apple. But wouldn't she be surprised in the morning when Isabelle presented her with a lovely, sweet chunk?

Isabelle tucked the partially eaten apple under her pillow. How easily she could have eaten the entire thing, stem, seeds, and all. How nice it would have felt in her stomach. But she was determined to share it with her friends.

She curled her legs beneath her only blanket. Tomorrow would bring another long day of peeling labels and pressing them onto boxes. Did they have factories in Nowhere? Did everyone in Nowhere grow mushrooms between their toes and lichen on their heads? Did apple trees . . . grow . . . and . . . plum . . . trees . . .

Sleep tugged at Isabelle's thoughts. But just as she closed her eyes, a scream shot up the stairway.

Chapter Five

THE HOODED STRANGER

Isabelle crept down the dark stairway, her bare feet gripping the cold planking. The Limewigs poked their heads out of their bedroom and whispered nervously as she hurried past. "Someone screamed."

The Wormbottoms huddled on the second floor's landing. "What's going on?" Mrs. Wormbottom asked. "Are we being robbed?"

"Don't go down there," Mr. Wormbottom said. "It might not be safe."

Curiosity is a powerful force, so Isabelle didn't heed his wise advice. She slipped between the Wormbottoms and continued down the stairs.

"You've ruined it!" Gertrude screeched. Light spilled from the kitchen. A cloud of black smoke drifted by. Isabelle tiptoed cautiously to the kitchen's entry and peeked around the wall.

The apple, now golden brown, sat in a pan on top of the oven. Sugar bubbled at its base and juice dripped from the hole where the stem used to be. A slice was missing.

"I didn't ruin it," Mama Lu insisted. "Look at it. It's perfect. Ya just got a bad slice. Try again."

Gertrude frowned. Oddly, her lips had turned black. The front of her bathrobe was black, too. She stuck a knife into the apple and carved another slice. Then she plunged a fork into the slice and held it at arm's length.

"That slice looks just fine. Go on. Give it a try," Mama Lu urged.

Watching those greedy women gobble up the beautiful baked apple would be torture, but Isabelle didn't turn away. Gertrude blew on the steaming slice and with a shaky hand, cautiously brought it to her mouth. But just as her blackened lips opened, the slice made a high-pitched sizzling sound. Then, *BAM!* It exploded. Gertrude screamed and dropped the fork. All that remained of the apple slice was a puff of black smoke.

Gertrude shook ash from her hair. "You ruined it," she snarled. "You overcooked my beautiful apple. You burnt it."

"It ain't overcooked," Mama Lu snarled right back. "Look at it." She pointed to the golden apple. "It ain't burnt one bit. I'll prove it." Mama Lu stuck a fork into the apple and lifted it from its pan. She didn't even bother to blow on it. She opened her mouth to take a great big bite.

Sizzle. SIZZLE. BAM!

This time both Mama Lu and Gertrude screamed as the apple exploded. The fork fell to the floor. Mama Lu's eyes popped even wider than the time she had found a family of slugs vacationing in her whipped cheese spread.

An enormous black cloud arose, blocking Isabelle's view. Coughing, the landladies ran from the kitchen straight into the parlor, where they gasped for air. Isabelle searched desperately for a hiding place and found it behind the hanging rain slickers. She snickered to herself, remembering Mama Lu's expression, then peered between yellow sleeves.

"You owe me an apple," Gertrude said, coughing.

"I owe ya nothing. That was a bad apple. Ain't my fault ya don't know the difference between a good apple and a bad apple."

"Are you calling me stupid?" Gertrude asked, shaking ashes from her bathrobe.

Mama Lu wiped soot from her eyes. "I ain't calling ya nothing. All I know is that it don't take much brains to know a bad apple is a bad apple."

Gertrude growled. "All I know is that it don't take much brains to know how to bake an apple."

"Are ya calling me a bad cook?"

They balled up their fists and stood, smudged face to smudged face. Isabelle delighted in the sight. They had gotten what they deserved for taking that apple from Gwen. Maybe they'd start punching each other. Oh, how she'd love to see that, but if the landladies caught her spying she'd be in huge trouble. How could she get back upstairs without being seen? The distance between the hanging slickers and the stairway stretched before her, where squeaky floorboards lay like landmines. It was too risky, but so was standing in the entryway with her feet sticking out from under the slickers.

Mama Lu's Boardinghouse had a back door, used only by Boris and Bert because it led directly to their basement room. Isabelle could hide in their room until Mama Lu went to sleep. She'd have to walk around to the back of the house in the dark, but she'd manage. The front door couldn't be seen from the parlor, so she'd be able to slip out. Isabelle reached for the knob and was about to yank it open when she noticed two eyes staring at her through the window.

"Ahhh!" she cried — not scared, just startled.

A stranger stood on the porch in a puddle of kitchen light. His eyes were darker than any eyes Isabelle had ever seen. And he wore a hooded cape.

"Who's that?" Mama Lu bellowed. Isabelle tried to hide behind the slickers again but Mama Lu grabbed her arm. "Whatcha doing down here? Ya looking fer something to steal?"

"No, I heard something. There's someone outside," Isabelle said, her heart pounding in her ears. "A stranger."

"What?" Mama Lu stomped over to the door and pulled it open. "There's no stranger out there." She slammed the door shut.

Gertrude emerged from the parlor, wiping soot off her face with her bathrobe sleeve. "She was going to steal my apple. That's why she came downstairs."

"I wasn't going to steal anything," Isabelle said. The landladies closed in. "There was a man standing on the porch just now. In a cape with a hood. I saw him."

"Yer a terrible liar. Did ya fiddle with my oven?" Mama Lu demanded. Isabelle shook her head. "I bet yer the reason the apple got ruined. She's the reason, Gertie. She thinks she's special just because she got left on a doorstep. Well, I say she's a mold-covered lying rat and she fiddled with my oven."

"You're right," Gertrude said. "She done it because she's friends with Gwen."

Isabelle braced herself for the inevitable punishment —
not a slap or a spanking, but a loss of a privilege.

"Ya know the rules," Mama Lu snarled, pointing a soot-
stained finger in Isabelle's face. "No walking around after
lights out. Ya just lost yer breakfast privileges."

"But . . ."

"And you'll have to pay for my apple," Gertrude said.
"Dish duty at my house for a whole month."

"But it wasn't *your* apple," Isabelle blurted. "The bird
didn't drop it on *your* head."

"Why, you little eavesdropping brat," Gertrude snarled.

Isabelle hadn't been in this much trouble since the broken
cheese tray incident. She needed a distraction. Just as Mama
Lu opened her blackened mouth to decree another punishment, Isabelle pointed at the fireplace where a tiny bit of
peat had fallen onto the hearth. "Slug," she said, trying to
sound alarmed.

"Slug?" Mama Lu cried. She drew the salt canister from
her bathrobe pocket and launched herself at the fireplace.
Snapping the canister open, she dumped the entire contents
onto the little peat ball.

"Kill it, kill it, kill it!" Gertrude screeched.

Isabelle raced up the stairs as fast as she could, fleeing the
wrath of the landladies.

It felt as if the stranger's dark gaze followed her every
step of the way.

Chapter Six
A SURPRISE FOR GWEN

The bedroom lights snapped back on at dawn. Isabelle hadn't slept a wink. How could she have, with visions of sneezing sea monsters, exploding apples, and strangers in hooded capes bouncing around in her head? She reached under her pillow and pulled out the partially eaten apple. Even though the flesh had turned brown, it still looked delicious. She took three huge bites. It still tasted delicious. How nice it would be to have an apple tree growing in the backyard! She could eat apples for breakfast, lunch, and dinner, or whenever the urge struck. How lucky her grandmother had been.

Wiping juice from her chin, Isabelle returned the apple to its hiding place. Grandma Maxine lay in a deep sleep, but she'd soon need breakfast, so Isabelle hurried downstairs with last night's tray.

The kitchen floor felt damp and slimy. Wind howled, rattling the panes. Raindrops beat a chaotic rhythm along the gutters. The tenants shuffled in, quiet and sleepy, taking their places at the table. Mr. Wormbottom rubbed his hands together to warm them. Mrs. Limewig held her cup of tea to her pallid cheek. Isabelle cleaned her grandmother's bowl and spoon at the sink.

"Good morning, Isabelle," Boris said.

"Good morning, Isabelle," Bert said.

Isabelle, sleepiest of all, returned their weak smiles, then filled her grandmother's bowl with cold, lumpy porridge. She poured tea into a cup.

"That food ain't fer you," Mama Lu barked from her throne. She had wrapped a knitted yellow scarf around her neck. A matching knitted yellow hat sat on her head like an oversized egg yolk. "Ya was up to no good last night so ya git nothing."

"I'm not eating anything," Isabelle said. "This is for my grandma." As much as Isabelle detested the porridge paste, her stomach already missed it.

"Yer a liar. Ya ruined my dessert," Mama Lu said, peeling orange wax from a wedge of cheese and flicking the bits onto her tenant's heads.

"I didn't ruin it," Isabelle blurted. "I didn't touch the apple. I came downstairs because I heard you scream."

"Is ya contradicting me? I say yer a liar."

"I'm not a liar." Isabelle held her breath, trying to control the anger that raced through her. What would the landlady do? Take away her breathing privileges? What else was there to take?

Mama Lu scowled and leaned over the armrest. The observation chair tipped precariously. "Don't make me come down there, you unwanted, abandoned little mushroom-growing wretch. 'Cause I will. I'll come down there and wallop ya on the head with my cheese tray."

Isabelle could see right up Mama Lu's gaping nostrils. She imagined climbing the observation chair's ladder and shoving a wedge of cheese right up that bulbous nose. But, of course, she didn't. She couldn't change the fact that Mama Lu was a tyrant or that her sick old grandmother needed breakfast. So, rather than defending herself further, she hummed a little song to calm herself down while she finished putting together the breakfast tray. And, since she had taught the song to the other tenants, they snickered while she hummed.

The Mama Lu Song

All day long she sits in her chair,
in her fuzzy bathrobe and striped underwear,
yelling and hollering and making up rules,
telling us we're stupid, calling us fools.
What can we do about Mama Lu?

We could
push over her chair,
stick slugs in her hair,
flush all of her cheese down the toilet.
Sneeze in her face,
track mud in the place,
take her bathrobe and boil it!

We could
dump gruel on her head,
put slugs in her bed,
fill both of her slippers with gutter sludge.

Give her a cold,
flick her with mold,
serve her slug poop and tell her it's fudge.

"Stop yer humming!" Mama Lu shouted. "Humming and singing all the time. Acting *different* and *special* all the time. Growing that stuff on yer head because ya thinks yer more important than anyone else."

Isabelle didn't think she was more important than anyone else, but she certainly knew that she was different — and that was a good thing, especially if it meant being different from Mama Lu. She picked up the breakfast tray and hurried from the kitchen, stepping over a new pile of salt. A brown puddle bubbled at the center of the pile.

Poor little slug.

One day, Isabelle hoped, the slugs of Runny Cove would rise up, form an army, and bury Mama Lu in a pile of slime so enormous that a person could dig for days and never find her.

Back upstairs, Isabelle decided not to wake her sleeping grandmother, so she set the tray on the bedside table, quickly warming the teacup in her hands. After checking on the barnacle, the slugs, and the potato bugs, she retrieved her apple. Using the spoon, she cut another chunk and left it on the breakfast tray. Then she cut four more chunks — one each for Bert, Boris, Leonard, and Gwen — and stuffed them into her shirt pocket. All that remained was the apple's core, which she ate in two bites, stem and all.

Take that, Mama Lu! I don't need your lumpy porridge.

As she chewed, something caught between her front teeth. She picked out a glossy black seed. How *interesting.*

BAROOO! The factory's horn rang across the village, warning workers that their shifts would begin in half an hour. Isabelle would have to wait to examine the seed — maybe during her lunch break. She tucked it into her sock so she wouldn't lose it along the way.

"Don't be late," Grandma Maxine muttered, opening her eyes.

"Are you feeling better?" Isabelle asked. "Do you need my help with the spoon?"

Grandma Maxine reached out her hand, which Isabelle took. "Yes, I'm feeling better. Go now or you'll be late." She closed her eyes again.

Her grandmother had never lied to her before. So, if she said she was feeling better then she must be, which was very good news. And yet, she looked as gray and shrunken as ever. "Be sure to eat all of it," Isabelle said, just before rushing out the door.

Boris and Bert sat on the entryway bench, pulling on their rubber boots. Mama Lu, still in her observation chair, was building a cheese tower, so she didn't notice when Isabelle slipped the apple chunks to the twins. Their blue eyes ignited mischievously. "Thank you," they whispered, happily gumming the fruit.

All along Boggy Lane, workers emerged from their boardinghouses. Slickers zipped to their chins, hoods tied securely, they formed a human stream. Fighting a strong headwind, they pushed their way through the village tired step after tired step, past the boarded-up schoolhouse and past the old fish market with its collapsed roof. They pushed past a vacant café and a vacant hardware store, ghosts from a time that only the old ones remembered. In the distance, the factory's cement towers pierced the low-hanging clouds.

Isabelle scanned the street, hoping to see the stranger so she could find out who he was. If he came from far away he might know about Nowhere. But alas, no sign of him.

Gwen waited outside Gertrude's Boardinghouse like she usually did. She and Isabelle walked behind the other workers so they wouldn't be overheard. "You won't believe what happened to me yesterday," she said, hooking her arm through Isabelle's. They pressed close, whispering beneath the rain's clatter.

"I know all about it. Gertrude brought your apple to Mama Lu's last night."

"She did?" Curls of gray hair fell across Gwen's sad eyes. She wiped her runny nose. "I hate Gertrude. I didn't get any breakfast because she said that I stole the apple. I didn't steal it." Her lower lip began to quiver. "I feel even sadder than I usually feel."

"I know you didn't steal the apple. But don't be sad. It turned black when Gertrude tried to eat it."

"Really? It turned black?" Gwen's mouth fell open.

"Yep. It exploded right in her face." Both girls giggled, a

rare sound in Runny Cove. "But there's more good news. Look." Isabelle reached beneath her slicker, into her shirt pocket, then handed Gwen a chunk. "I got an apple too, but mine didn't explode."

Gwen didn't bother asking questions. She eagerly popped the chunk into her mouth. "It's sooooo good."

As they walked, and as Gwen chewed, Isabelle told her about the sea monster with the dangly nose and about Leonard's cat.

"That's so weird," Gwen said.

"It's the strangest thing that's ever happened."

"Except for you being left on a doorstep."

"Yeah. Except for that." Isabelle wiped rain from her eyes. "We need to talk to Leonard. Maybe he knows something we don't."

They turned off Soaked Street and started up the steep gravel road that led to the factory. Suddenly, an eerie sensation crept over Isabelle, tickling the back of her neck, but not in a nice way. Why did she feel as if someone was watching her?

"Gwen?"

"Yeah?" Gwen wiped a slug from her sleeve.

"There was this man wearing a cape, standing on Gertrude's porch last night. Does she have a new tenant?"

"No. Maybe she has a new *boyfriend.*" Gwen rolled her eyes and pretended to upchuck. Isabelle giggled again. They loved making fun of Gertrude's boyfriend, Mr. Hench.

Whenever he kissed Gertrude, the slurping sound was so loud it seemed as if he might suck her face right off.

BEEP, BEEP.

Startled, Isabelle and Gwen scampered to the roadside, expecting a delivery truck to pass by. Trucks delivered supplies to the factory store, the only place in Runny Cove to buy food and sundries. Trucks hauled boxed umbrellas from the factory, taking them to towns that the workers had never seen.

BEEP, BEEP.

But it wasn't a truck. Mr. Supreme's sleek black roadster sped up the road. The license plate read: IMRICH. Mr. Supreme occasionally visited Runny Cove to inspect his factory. He didn't live in the village. He didn't have to.

BAROOO!

The factory's horn sounded the five-minute warning. Mr. Supreme's roadster churned up mud, splattering the fronts of the girls' rain slickers. He neither stopped to apologize nor offered the girls a ride. He didn't care about manners. He didn't need to.

"We'd better hurry," Isabelle said, coughing from the thick exhaust fumes.

The girls ran toward the factory.

And as they ran, the seed, still tucked inside Isabelle's sock, began to vibrate.

Chapter Seven
MR. SUPREME

After hanging up their slickers and tying their grimy aprons around their waists, the girls lined up with the other workers along the wall of a huge cement room. The apple seed continued to vibrate, just enough to make Isabelle want to scratch her leg. Mr. Hench stood on his security balcony. A metal badge shone on his gray uniform. Isabelle tapped her boot on the water-stained floor, trying to shake the seed into a less itchy position. Leonard stood at the far end of the line. *I can hardly wait to tell him,* she thought. He waved but there wasn't time to give him the apple chunk. Mr. Supreme had sauntered into the room. Everyone froze.

Mr. Supreme handed his black umbrella to one of his many sniveling assistants — a nameless cluster of men who wore long white coats and stuck to the boss like barnacles. Mr. Supreme plunked a yellow hard hat on his head, then dropped a cigar stump onto the floor. His glossy black trench coat crunched as he walked up and down the line, twirling his driving gloves as if he didn't have a care in the world. Perhaps he didn't. Perhaps having lots of money made it possible to live a life without worry.

Isabelle didn't like Mr. Supreme, not because he sprayed mud on girls without apologizing, but because he was stingy. As owner of the Magnificently Supreme Umbrella factory, he controlled the paychecks of almost every person in Runny Cove and he barely paid them enough to survive. As owner of the only store in Runny Cove, he supplied life's necessities — except for umbrellas. Never, ever did Mr. Supreme's Factory store sell umbrellas. Therefore, the people who actually made the umbrellas never got to use them, and that made no sense to Isabelle.

With Gwen and Leonard's help, Isabelle had made up a little song about Mr. Supreme. As he sneered at his employees, the song ran through her head.

The Mr. Supreme Song

We work in your factory all day,
in exchange for our pitiful pay.
But what would we do if we didn't have you?
Three jeers for Mr. Supreme
(he's a stinker),
three jeers for Mr. Supreme.

You seem like a mean sort of fella,
standing under your big black umbrella.
But what would we do if we didn't have you?
Three jeers for Mr. Supreme
(he's a pooper),
three jeers for Mr. Supreme.

Mr. Supreme, Mr. Supreme,
I bet your life is just like a dream.

**With your boots and cigars and your big fancy cars,
you're a stinker, Mr. Supreme.**

Gwen gave Isabelle a sharp poke with her elbow. "You're humming too loud," she whispered.

Up and down the line the boss strode, smiling smugly at the quivering workers. "Good morning, Magnificently Supreme Factory Employees." His voice rolled across the cement room like a tsunami.

"Good morning, Mr. Supreme, sir," the workers chanted.

Isabelle shook her leg. That seed was driving her nuts.

He halted, resting his hands behind his back, and cleared his throat disapprovingly. "I couldn't hear you."

"GOOD MORNING, MR. SUPREME, SIR!"

"That's better, but not good enough." He stuck out his cleft chin. "So, let's try that again. Good morning, Magnificently Supreme Factory Employees." He put his hand to his ear.

The workers screamed, "GOOD MORNING, MAGNIFICENTLY SUPREME FACTORY EMPLOYEES!" Then they put their hands to their ears.

Mr. Supreme frowned. "Stupidest bunch of workers I've got," he murmured to one of his assistants.

"Stupidest," the assistant agreed.

The boss stuffed his driving gloves into his pocket. "I have something glorious to show you," he announced to the workers. "Something that will insure my factory's future and thus, *your* futures." He clapped his hands together.

A smallish assistant scurried in, carrying a closed umbrella. Before taking the umbrella, Mr. Supreme whipped a canister from his pocket. It didn't read: SALT, like Mama Lu's canister. Rather, it read: ANTIBACTERIAL WIPES. He proceeded to wipe down the umbrella's handle. "Magnificently Supreme Factory Employees, behold the future."

Mr. Supreme held the closed umbrella above his head. Isabelle and Gwen exchanged shrugs. It looked like the same black metal-framed umbrella the factory had produced for as long as they could remember. What could possibly be glorious about a black umbrella?

Mr. Supreme pulled off the umbrella's black sheath and pushed a little lever. The umbrella swooshed open. Transfixed, no one moved. No one breathed. Then a chorus of "Ahhhh," and "Ooooh," echoed off the cement walls. For what had appeared to be an ordinary black umbrella was neither ordinary nor black. Radiant red, brighter than the mysterious apples, shone above Mr. Supreme's head.

A trio of assistants hurried around the room, handing umbrellas to the workers. "These are the prototypes. Open them!" Mr. Supreme exclaimed.

Swoosh, swoosh, swoosh.

Isabelle removed her umbrella's cover and pressed the lever. Royal purple erupted above her head. Silver beads dangled from the umbrella's edges, tinkling magically. Gwen basked beneath gold, Mr. Wormbottom beneath amber. Mrs. Wormbottom twirled a turquoise number with yellow tassels. Lime, silver, chocolate, and vanilla danced in the air.

The usually colorless faces of the factory's workers reflected the umbrella colors in a way that was both awesome and terrifying. Everyone started talking at once.

Isabelle closed her umbrella and darted between the excited workers. Sure, she felt as amazed as they did, but she had something more important on her mind.

"Leonard," she called. Leonard's entire face, including his birthmark, glowed as pink as the umbrella he stood beneath. Some people called him ugly, but Isabelle was so used to the birthmark she barely noticed it. "Here." She pulled the apple chunk from her shirt pocket. "Don't let anyone see. It's from an apple. It's for you."

Like Gwen, Leonard popped the chunk into his mouth.

"Tell me about your apple," she said.

He swallowed. "Huh? How did you know about it?"

"Mr. Hench told Gertrude." Isabelle bounced on her toes, as much from excitement as from that pesky seed. "I don't have time to explain. Just tell me, did you really find it under a cat?"

"Yeah." He lowered his umbrella, sheltering them beneath its rosy glow. "A big orange cat. Hench called me a thief and took the apple. But when he tried to eat it, the apple turned black."

"Really?"

"Back in line, everyone!" Mr. Supreme called.

Darn it. Isabelle had so many questions. "We'll talk at lunch," she told Leonard.

"Okay," he said. He raised the umbrella and Isabelle scurried to her place.

Mr. Supreme climbed the stairs to the security guard's balcony and looked down upon the glowing faces of his workers. "Black umbrellas are no longer in fashion," he declared. "Black umbrellas are outdated. No one wants a black umbrella anymore."

Every worker in Runny Cove would have loved to own a black umbrella.

"My clients, people of the highest caliber and breeding who live far, far from this revolting place, want umbrellas to match their shoes and umbrellas to match their traveling cases. Umbrellas to match their frocks and umbrellas to match their dog's frocks. Some want a different color umbrella for each day of the week."

Isabelle furrowed her brow. Why would a person need so many umbrellas? What did it matter what an umbrella looked like, as long as it kept the rain off?

"Of course," Mr. Supreme said, "this will mean extra work for everyone." A low groan rolled across the room as workers reacted to his announcement. Mr. Supreme pulled a wipe from his canister and dabbed his forehead. "Extra work to begin immediately."

This was terrible news. Impossible news. How could she work extra hours when she was already working extra hours? She couldn't. She'd have to tell him. What choice did she have? "Excuse me, sir," Isabelle said, timidly raising her hand.

"What's that?" Mr. Supreme asked, adjusting his hard hat.

"It appears to be a little girl, sir," replied an assistant.

"A little girl?" He leaned over the balcony. "What do you want, little girl?"

Isabelle had never spoken directly to Mr. Supreme. But no one else could excuse her from extra, extra hours. Though she shook like a windowpane in a windstorm, Isabelle stepped forward. "I'm already working extra hours to pay my rent because my Grandma Maxine is sick. And I have to do dish duty at Gertrude's house for the next month because she thinks I burnt her apple. If I work even more hours then I'll get home too late to feed my grandmother. I don't think . . ." She paused. What she was about to say had never been said. "I don't think . . ."

"What don't you think?"

The seed's vibrations increased, matching her own trembling. "I don't think I can work more hours."

The workers let the umbrellas fall to their sides. Isabelle's heart thumped wildly in her chest as Mr. Supreme eyed her in the same way that a crow might eye a wiggling worm. He tapped his boot irritably. "I will overlook your insolence, little girl, because you are too young to understand the significance of the Magnificently Supreme Umbrella Factory. But the older workers understand." A few workers nodded. "They remember that after all the fish had died and all the ships had rotted from disuse, they were starving and near death. But my grandfather, Mr. Supreme Senior, built this factory and gave them jobs despite their feeble constitutions and below-average intellects." The sleeves of his coat crunched as he folded his arms. "So, little girl, when I tell you that you must work extra hours, I expect gratitude. Of course, you are always free to look elsewhere for work. Perhaps everyone would like to look elsewhere for work?" He shared a chuckle with his assistants, because, after all, there was no place else to work in Runny Cove.

"We will work," the workers called out.

Tears floated at the edges of Isabelle's eyes. "Thank you, sir. Thank you for the extra hours." She stepped back into line. Gwen reached out and squeezed her hand.

"Now that that bit of unpleasantry has passed, I'm pleased to announce that the new colorful dyes have already arrived," Mr. Supreme said. "I'm going to make a fortune on these new umbrellas, so get to work, everyone."

The assistants collected the colorful umbrellas as the workers shuffled off to their stations. Isabelle waved a sad good-bye to Leonard and Gwen and headed to the labeling room on the main floor. Her tears soon cleared but the seed continued to drive her mad. As soon as she got to her station, she reached into her sock and pulled it out. It bounced inside her cupped hand like a sand flea. Where could she put it?

The conveyor belt clunked and began its slow roll. A box appeared, winding toward Isabelle's station. She needed both hands to stick the labels. Each label read: MAGNIFICENTLY SUPREME UMBRELLAS — SUPREME RAIN COVERS FOR THOSE WITH SUPREME TASTE.

The box rolled closer. Isabelle didn't want to lose the strange seed. It seemed as if her sock would be the safest place. She'd simply have to endure the tickling. She was about to tuck it in when she noticed a little white root sticking out one end. It had sprouted. But that was not all.

It was humming happily between her warm palms.

Once again, an eerie sensation tickled Isabelle's neck. She knew, even before she turned to make certain, that the hooded stranger was peering at her through the factory window.

Chapter Eight
BIG TROUBLE

The factory horn blew at four hours past the usual quitting time. The extra work had cut into the lunch break so there had been no opportunity for Isabelle to talk to her friends. But while the day had moved as slowly as an over-fed slug, Isabelle's thoughts had bounced along with the seed's rhythm.

Do not forget that Isabelle's head was already full of un-answered questions like *Where did I come from?* and *Why am I different?* Now a mess of new questions shoved their way in, screaming, *Answer me! Answer me!* Questions like, *Why did the stranger disappear again? Why was he staring at me? Why did that sea monster have such an odd nose? Was Grandma Maxine really feeling better? Why would a bird drop an apple onto someone's head? Do most apple seeds jump and hum?* Just to mention a few.

It was getting crowded in Isabelle's head.

Workers zipped up their slickers, tied their hoods, and headed into the gloomy night. Flickering village lights guided them home. "Hey, Isabelle," Leonard called out, waving. But his parents grabbed his arms.

"Stay away from her," his dad said. "She almost got every-one fired." They pulled him into the crowd.

Gwen took Isabelle's hand. "Don't worry. They won't be mad at you tomorrow. Remember the shipping incident. They forgave you after a few days."

The "shipping incident" had taken place the prior year,

long before Grandma Maxine had become ill. The friends had argued over who should go but in the end Leonard was chosen because he was shorter than Gwen and Isabelle, and thus, could better fit into a box. After shutting and taping the box, Isabelle had written TO NOWHERE on the shipping label. Once he had arrived, Leonard was supposed to take a good look around and then ship himself back.

But the box never made it past Mr. Supreme's assistants on account of the air holes and Leonard's snickering.

The girls started down the muddy road. Isabelle's feet ached worse than ever. "We've got to hurry," she said to Gwen. "My grandma needs her dinner."

"I still can't believe you actually talked to Mr. Supreme."

"I had to. Please, can't you walk faster?" Isabelle asked.

Gwen stopped. "I'm too tired. My legs are killing me. You go on." She gave Isabelle a weak hug. "See ya in the morning."

"See ya."

Isabelle took off at a full run. She was the first of Mama Lu's tenants to arrive home. She didn't have to slam her body against the stubborn front door because it stood wide open — which was highly unusual. Rain fell into the entry-way. The kitchen sat quiet. No cabbage soup bubbled. No one hollered, "Did ya check fer slugs?"

Something is wrong.

A series of thumps and bumps sounded above.

Isabelle took the stairs, racing up one flight, then the next. She didn't even slow down for the super steep third flight. Her bedroom door also stood wide open. Shredded clumps of moss lay in the hallway. Something flew out of the bedroom and landed with a splat against the wall.

"SLUUUUUG!"

Isabelle plugged her ears as the screech repeated.

"SLUUUUUG!"

Mama Lu stomped out of the room on the fourth floor and stood, blocking the entry. Her fuzzy bathrobe hung open; her striped long johns clung to ripples of cheese-fed fat. Her face was all scrunched up like a wadded towel. In one hand she held the slug garden, in the other her canister of salt. "SLUUUUUG!" she wailed as she poured salt over the garden. The poor creatures had no chance of escape.

"No!" Isabelle cried.

"YOU!" Mama Lu tossed the garden aside, then stomped back into the bedroom. Isabelle knelt beside the cracker box, hoping to find survivors, but Mama Lu reappeared in the doorway with the potato bug palace.

"Please don't hurt them," Isabelle begged.

Mama Lu scrunched her face even tighter. It turned bright red. "Ya did this. Ya brought these vermin into my house. Who do ya think ya are? This is *my* home." She overturned the milk carton. The bugs fell onto the floor and immediately curled into balls. Mama Lu raised her slipper.

"Oh no. Please, no."

Mama Lu stomped them flat. "Vermin. Nasty vermin."

Isabelle trembled from head to foot. She wanted to fling herself at Mama Lu. She wanted to push the horrid woman down the stairs. But she and her grandmother had nowhere else to go.

"Ya want these bugs to crawl into my ear while I sleep? Ya want me to slip on slug slime?"

YES! Isabelle wanted to scream. She grabbed a twig, onto which a few bugs clung. "Please stop. I'll put them back outside. Just stop hurting them."

"And what about them plants? What do ya think likes to live on plants? Slugs and bugs, that's what. If God had intended plants to be inside, He wouldn't have put them outside. Yer in big trouble." She grabbed the twig and stomped it flat.

Poor little bugs.

Grandma Maxine would be worried, what with all the hollering and stomping. Isabelle tried to squeeze past her evil landlady but Mama Lu grabbed her by the hood. "I said, yer in big trouble."

"Let me go." Isabelle squirmed but the landlady's grip held fast.

Boris and Bert appeared at the top of the stairs, with the Wormbottoms and Limewigs right behind. "Is something wrong?" Boris asked timidly.

"She's what's wrong," Mama Lu said. "Always has been something wrong with this girl."

"Let me go," Isabelle cried, flailing and swinging her arms. "I want to see my grandma."

"Ain't no use seeing her." Mama Lu let go of the hood. " 'Cause she's dead. Ya hear me? Dead."

Chapter Nine

ESCAPE FROM
RUNNY COVE

Every once in a while time decides to stand still. And that is what it did as Isabelle took in those dreadful words. Her heart stopped mid-beat; her breath froze. Only the moment existed — the moment between the old life that she had known and the new life that she didn't want to know. If only she could stay in that moment forever and never face the truth . . . but the gasps of the other tenants pulled her into reality. Unbearable reality.

Isabelle rushed into the bedroom. Grandma Maxine's bed lay empty; her tattered quilt had fallen to the floor. The bed sheet still held the outline of her grandmother's body. "Where is she?" Isabelle cried.

Mama Lu followed her into the bedroom, as did the tenants. "I told ya, she's dead." Her tone held no sympathy, as if Grandma Maxine were as insignificant as a dead bug. "And it was about time she died, doing no work, getting her meals served to her. This ain't no hospital. She was a deadbeat, that's what she was."

The room tilted. Isabelle felt woozy. Bert rushed forward and took her arm. "Poor little Isabelle," he cooed.

Boris took the other arm. "We're so sorry, Isabelle."

"Whatcha sorry fer?" Mama Lu bellowed.

Isabelle couldn't pull her gaze from the sheet. "But . . . where is she?"

"Undertaker took her." Mama Lu tore a vine from the

wall, exposing a cracked wallboard. A cold breeze immediately seeped through. "It's gonna cost a lot of money to fix this room." She pointed a finger in Isabelle's face. "And yer paying every cent. Ya hear me?" Mama Lu cared more about a room than about the fact that one of her tenants had just died!

Isabelle threw herself across her grandmother's bed, trying to hide her tears.

"We'll help her pay," Boris said.

"Us too," said the Wormbottoms.

"No one pays but her," Mama Lu snarled. "She's the one who done this. Bringing slugs and plants into my house 'cause she thinks she's so special. Well, I got news fer ya. Ya ain't special. Ya was thrown away, just like garbage." With a loud grunt, she tore another vine. "She and her granny was always my worst tenants. Always late on their rent. Always eating more food than they needed. But me, being kind-hearted, allowed them to stay."

Lies, lies, LIES!

Isabelle pushed herself off the bed. "Get out!" she cried. Uncontrollable rage pounded in her head. "This is my room. Get out of here. Leave me alone!"

"How dare ya yell at me."

"She's dead and you don't even care." Isabelle balled up her fists, ready to wallop Mama Lu if she kept saying mean things. "She's dead and you don't . . ." Isabelle hesitated.

At that moment, her mind cleared and she realized that, like so many recent events, this one didn't make sense.

Something wasn't right. She pointed a finger in Mama Lu's face. "How did you know she was dead?" she asked. "You never come up to the fourth floor and we were at the factory. How did you know?"

Mama Lu tied her bathrobe around her enormous middle. "The undertaker told me, dimwit. He knocked on the door and told me."

"But how did the undertaker know? Who would have called him?"

"How am I supposed to know that?" Mama Lu kicked at a clump of moss. "And why would I care? He said she was dead and he took her away. Now don't try to change the subject. Yer not getting any meals until this entire room is scrubbed clean."

"But how . . . ?"

"Shut yer trap. She's dead, ya hear? And I've come to collect her belongings."

So there it was, the only reason why Mama Lu would heave herself up three flights of stairs — greed, pure and simple. The landlady yanked open Grandma Maxine's bedside drawer, which held bits and pieces of her life — a pair of knitting needles, some buttons, a chipped teacup, a pair of socks, to name just a few.

"Those belong to me," Isabelle said as Mama Lu stuffed the bits and pieces into her bathrobe pockets.

"This stuff is mine 'cause it's in my house. It don't belong to you 'cause she weren't yer *real*, blood-born granny. But don't think fer a minute that this will pay off yer debt.

You'll be workin' fer months to pay fer all the damage done to this room."

Tears welled in Isabelle's eyes. How could she work more?

Boris stepped forward. "I got an extra dollar."

"I got an extra dollar, too," said Mr. Limewig.

"Shut yer traps, all of ya. This ain't none of yer business. Go on, get out of here." She shoved the tenants into the hallway and down the stairs. Then she returned for Isabelle. "I've been far too nice to ya, lettin' ya sleep in this luxurious room. Ya'll sleep on the porch from now on."

Isabelle turned away. She was not going to let the landlady see her tears. *I didn't get the chance to say goodbye. Now I'm an orphan, like Gwen.*

The seed, which had been quietly resting inside Isabelle's sock, chose that moment to start humming like a trapped housefly.

"Is ya singing again?" Mama Lu asked. She stared at Isabelle's rubber boot. "What ya got in there?"

"Nothing." Isabelle wiped her eyes.

"That ain't nothing. Whatever it is, give it over."

"No." Isabelle's knees started to tremble.

"Give it, I say. It's my house. Them's my rules."

Isabelle felt so scared she thought she might fall over. "No. You can't have it."

"Ya little brat!" Mama Lu tried to grab a clump of Isabelle's hair but she wasn't quick enough. "Ya'll do what I say or ya won't be living here no more."

"I don't want to live here anymore," Isabelle cried, backing toward the door. "I'll go live with Gwen."

"No ya won't. Gertrude won't take ya 'cause I won't let her. Ya owe me too much money."

"Then I'll live somewhere else. I'll go to another town, far, far away." Nothing was keeping her in Runny Cove. She couldn't work enough hours to satisfy Mr. Supreme, Gertrude, *and* Mama Lu. And without her grandmother, no one needed her.

Mama Lu reached into the bedside drawer again and found some buttons. "There's nothing out there fer ya. Yer just a stupid factory worker."

The seed hummed louder. Isabelle tried to look brave. She held up her chin. "I'm going to find out where I came from."

"Where ya came from?" Mama Lu snorted. She pulled the drawer free and shook it over the bed. She had taken everything. "Ya came from noplace. Now, give me whatever's in yer boot."

All that had been beautiful about the room on the fourth floor was gone — the happy stories of Sunny Cove, the peaceful little creatures, the warm mossy carpet and the glistening vines. But one little thing remained — one creature that had eluded Mama Lu's stomping foot.

"Give me yer boot!" Mama Lu lunged at Isabelle. At that moment, Isabelle felt a bolt of courage. She ducked beneath Mama Lu's swinging arm and grabbed the pickle jar aquarium.

"I hate you," she cried. "You're mean and you smell like stinky cheese. And I hate this place. I came from Nowhere and I'm going to find it." She rushed into the hallway.

"Stop her!" Mama Lu screamed. "Thief! That's my pickle jar."

"It's mine. You threw it away." The aquarium water sloshed as Isabelle stumbled down the stairs. The tenants huddled on the third-floor landing, their gloomy faces gloomier than ever.

"Good luck," Mrs. Wormbottom said, a tear in her eye.

"Take care of yourself," Mr. Limewig said, his voice cracking with emotion.

Isabelle wanted to hug and kiss each one of them but there was no time. Mama Lu's footsteps thundered close behind.

"Nothing leaves this house without my permission. She's a thief! Someone call Mr. Hench!"

"You'll get arrested if you take that," Boris said, pointing at the aquarium.

"I won't let her kill my barnacle. Grandma taught me all about barnacles."

"Then we'll try to slow her down," Bert said. "Hurry."

"Thank you. Goodbye," Isabelle called as she flew down the last two flights.

"Stop! Ya'll go to jail, ya moldy little thief! Get out of my way!" Mama Lu screamed. "Ya stupid dunderheads is blocking the stairs!"

Rain poured as Isabelle leapt off the front porch. Oh, how she wanted to tell Gwen that she was leaving, but she couldn't risk slowing down. "Goodbye, Gwen!" she yelled as she passed Gertrude's Boardinghouse, hoping her friend might hear. "I'll send word as soon as I get there."

Water splashed into her boots as she ran up Boggy Lane. Kitchen lights reflected in the ankle-deep water. Mama Lu would soon ring Mr. Hench and he'd come looking for her. "Goodbye, Leonard," she called as she passed his boarding-house.

At the edge of town she stopped running. Out of breath and coughing, she set down the aquarium and rested her hands on her knees. Which way should she go? The gravel road stretched before her, its right fork leading to the factory, its left fork winding through miles of dangerous bogs and swamps. Only the heavy-duty headlights of Mr. Supreme's delivery trucks could cut through the bog's thick fog. The older villagers often said that the few who had tried to leave Runny Cove on foot either drowned in swamp mud or got eaten alive by swamp frogs.

Isabelle looked over her shoulder. No one had followed. Not yet. She tried not to think about her grandmother. She tried to focus on her escape. But again and again the words repeated: *She's dead. Ya hear me? Dead.*

Suddenly, Isabelle ached to see her grandmother one last time. But the cemetery would be an obvious place to search for Mama Lu's thief. Grandma Maxine wouldn't be able to hear the goodbye anyway. All that remained was her body.

"A body is just a container," Mrs. Wormbottom had once told Isabelle. "When we die, our body is left behind but our soul goes on a journey to a wonderful place."

If Grandma Maxine's soul had gone on a journey to a *wonderful place*, then it would certainly have gone as far away from Runny Cove as possible.

Isabelle took a deep, decisive breath. Hugging the pickle jar, she started across the dunes. The factory's yellow lights cast an eerie haze upon the sand. The rain poured as she negotiated the slippery driftwood, but both she and the barnacle reached the beach without injury.

The wind stung with needles of icy seawater as Isabelle scurried down the beach. With each step the factory's lamplight faded and the abandoned fishing boats took on eerie shapes. She had never walked beyond the cove and when she reached its edge, fear crept over her. She rounded the rocky bluff and stared into total darkness. Not even Runny Cove eyes can cut through total darkness. She'd have to wait for morning light.

A boat lay up the beach, half-buried in the sand. The cabin door had long fallen free. With an outstretched hand she found a corner bunk, its wooden slats still strong enough to hold her. Suddenly, sadness weighed down every part of her body. She set the aquarium onto the sandy floor, then lay on the bunk and tucked her knees to her chest. She tried to keep the bad thoughts away, tried not to think of Mama Lu, or the undertaker, or holes in the ground where dead bodies are buried. She shivered as dampness seeped into her clothing. She trembled as grief took hold. For the first time in her memory, Isabelle had no one.

No one to answer her questions. No one to tell her stories of the old days. No one to say, "Good night, Isabelle."

And that's when the apple seed began to hum again. Not like a trapped insect, but a sort of melody, as if it were making up its own little song. She picked the seed out of her sock. The melody traveled up her arm. It spread over her chest and down her other arm until it had covered her entire body like a blanket. The song continued, soft and comforting, like a grandmother's sweet humming. As Isabelle held the seed between her palms, her eyelids grew heavy and the bad thoughts drifted away.

Many hours later, Isabelle opened her eyes. She thought at first that she was dreaming because she saw the following things: a small fire flickering in the center of the boat's cabin, an orange cat lounging beside the fire, and a black bird nibbling on a piece of bread.

And last but not least, a figure wearing a hooded cape, stirring a cup of something that smelled wonderful.

Chapter Ten

A BOY NAMED SAGE

The stranger sat so close that Isabelle could hear the liquid swirling inside his mug. She clamped her eyes shut and pretended to still be asleep, then slowed her breathing and snored a few times, for good measure. She had hoped to see him again, to ask him if he had come from Nowhere, but now that he sat nearby she felt a bit afraid. Grandma Maxine had told her never to trust a stranger. "Sometimes," she had said, "strangers are dangerous."

The bird squawked.

"I know," the stranger said, not in a deep, scary voice as one might imagine would come from a cloaked person, but in a youngish, soft voice. Who was he talking to?

The bird squawked again.

"I heard you," the stranger replied. "I know Isabelle's awake. She'll speak to us when she's ready."

Isabelle opened her eyes and sat up. The stranger kept his back to her. If he tried to hurt her, the cabin entrance was just a quick dash away. Only the cat lay in her path, stretched out as limp as an orange scarf. Isabelle slid to the edge of the bunk. The black bird squawked again and flew across the cabin, landing beside her leg. It cocked its head and pecked at her hand. "Hey," she cried as it tried to snatch the seed from her palm. The bird pecked again, this time pinching her skin. "Stop it."

The stranger turned. "Leave the seed, Rolo." Then he pushed off his hood.

Isabelle gasped. "You're just a kid."

"A kid?" He glared at her, clearly insulted. "I'm twelve. I'm not a *kid.*"

"Oh. I'm not a kid either." She tried to sound tough.

"Well, you look like a kid. Look how short you are." He, on the other hand, wasn't one bit short. And his skin wasn't translucent, but as brown as wet driftwood. His hair wasn't normal either, for it hung in long tangled ropes and was black rather than gray.

"Were you talking to that bird?" Isabelle asked.

"Yep. We talk to each other all the time."

"That's kind of weird."

"Not as weird as carrying a barnacle around in a pickle jar." He offered the mug to her. "You can have some of this."

"What is it?"

"Cinnamon tea. Go on. It'll help you wake up. You've got a long journey ahead of you."

How did he know about her journey? Isabelle's mouth felt dry. Too bad she hadn't grabbed a water bottle just before her escape from Mama Lu's. But maybe it wouldn't be a good idea to drink tea from a stranger. "I don't want any tea. I mean, no thank you."

"Suit yourself." He tucked one of the tangled ropes behind his ear, then took a long sip from the mug. "I don't really like tea that much. But it's easy to travel with."

The seed started vibrating so fast that it stung Isabelle's hand. She winced. The bird stared intently, clicking its beak.

"Your apple seed is ready for planting," the boy said. He reached into a green satchel and removed a small fabric bag. "If you put it into this light-proof bag it will sleep."

Isabelle cautiously accepted the bag and dropped the seed inside. Sure enough, it stopped vibrating. She tied the string and tucked the bag into her slicker's pocket.

Birds can talk and seeds can sleep. How very *interesting*.

"How did you know I had an apple seed?"

"Because I delivered the apples." The boy took another sip.

"No you didn't." Aha! She had caught him in a lie and liars shouldn't be trusted. She folded her arms, waiting for his explanation.

"Okay, well, technically an elephant seal delivered your apple. But I'm the one who told the seal to deliver it." He reached into his satchel and pulled out some bread. Isabelle's stomach growled at the sight of the golden loaf. He tore the bread in half. The inside looked soft and fluffy. The bird flew onto the boy's shoulder and accepted a morsel of crust.

Isabelle had never tasted fluffy bread. She tried to ignore her moaning stomach. "An elephant seal? Is that what the sea monster is called?"

"Actually, his name is Neptune."

"He has a name?"

The boy stared, bewildered. "Everyone has a name. Don't you know that? My name is Sage. The raven's name is Rolo and the cat's name is Eve."

At the sound of her name, the cat began to purr. She raised her head and winked lazily at Isabelle.

Sage held out one of the halves, offering it to Isabelle. "It's not poisoned or anything. I'm not here to kill you. I'm here to collect you. Go on, eat this. You'll need food in your belly." He took a bite. "See. It's good."

Her willpower dissolved. She grabbed the bread and sank her teeth into its airy center. She took another bite and another.

Sage smiled. "Don't they ever feed you in that boarding-house?"

"Not enough," she replied with a full mouth. A crumb fell to her feet and was quickly pilfered by the raven.

"I suppose you have a lot of questions," Sage said, adding a piece of driftwood to the fire. The smoke trailed out the open doorway.

Isabelle nodded, her stuffed cheeks bulging like two apples, but the questions could wait for just a few more bites, surely. She stuffed, chewed, and swallowed, eating as ravenously as Mama Lu and Gertrude after one of their failed diets.

Sage drank the last of his tea. "I can't explain everything because there isn't much time. Dawn will be here soon and we need to leave on the morning tide. But I'll tell you what I can."

As the fire flickered and the rain fell on the cabin's roof, Sage spoke quickly. "As I told you, my name is Sage. I traveled down the mountains and across the ocean to find you. All I knew was that ten years ago a baby was left in this awful place but I didn't know if the baby was a boy or a girl. So I sent Rolo to scout around. He learned that there were only three kids in Runny Cove who were ten years old. So I brought the three apples and Rolo, Eve, and Neptune helped me deliver them to the three kids. Then I waited to see which one of you was the tender." He stopped, as if he had explained everything.

Isabelle wiped her mouth, more confused than ever. "Was the what?"

"The tender. Turned out to be you. You're a tender."

"Me?"

"Yes, you. One day, you might be the last tender in the whole world."

Nothing he had said made any sense. Maybe he was crazy like Mr. Morris, the man who sometimes danced naked in the rain.

"I'm sorry but you've gotten me mixed up with someone else. I'm just Isabelle. I'm a box labeler. I work at the umbrella factory."

Sage shook his head, his expression somber. "There's no mistake. The apple seed is living proof. Only a tender can make the apple seed grow. It's an odd sort of apple."

Isabelle leaned forward. "What do you mean?"

"It's a Love Apple," he said, stroking the cat's back. "Only

85

someone with a pure heart can eat a Love Apple. That's why it turned black when Mama Lu and Gertrude tried to eat one and when Mr. Hench tried to eat one. Love Apples know the difference."

"They do?" Isabelle leaned farther.

"Sure. That's their purpose. But the seed, well, that's another story entirely. Only a tender can germinate a Love Apple's seed. It has something to do with the fact that a tender's hands are extra warm."

Isabelle held out her hands and looked at them as if she had never seen them before.

Sage tucked the mug into his satchel. Then he stood and brushed sand off his cape. "Tenders grow things."

Isabelle frowned, lowering her hands. How disappointing. He had the wrong person after all. "Well, that proves that I'm not a tender because I don't grow things."

He frowned. "Of course you grow things. Look at your room and your locker at work. And your body. You've got lichen growing in your hair and I bet you can grow mushrooms between your toes. Only a tender can do that."

"But those things grow by themselves," Isabelle explained, scratching a patch of mold at the back of her neck.

"Stop being so dense," he said irritably. "You're a tender." And then he said the magic word. "Tenders are *special*."

Isabelle had never known the sensation of standing beneath clouds at the very moment when they part and the sun breaks through — but that is how she felt. Her entire body tingled. "I'm *special*?" she whispered.

"Tenders are incredibly special. Only a few people get to be tenders. I wish I could be one." He sighed. "But those are enough questions for now. Dawn's almost here. We need to go."

"Go?" Isabelle wanted to talk more about being special. "Are you going to Nowhere, too?"

"Nowhere?"

"That's where I'm from. But I don't think I should go with you. I don't even know you."

He folded his arms. "Actually, it's not called Nowhere. And if you don't know the correct name then how will you get there? You don't have any supplies or anything. And which way will you go? The mountains that lie to the north will freeze you to death and the desert that lies to the south will cook you to death." He smirked. "So? Which way will you go?"

Isabelle wrung her hands. Which way was north? Which way south? Dreaming about a journey was entirely different from actually taking that journey. Maybe she was the crazy one. No one but Mr. Supreme's delivery truck drivers had ever left Runny Cove. What had she done? Going back meant work, work, work. No way did she want to spend another day standing beside that clunking conveyor belt. No way did she want to set foot in Mama Lu's Boardinghouse again. Going back meant possible imprisonment for taking Mama Lu's pickle jar. Going forward could mean freezing like an ice cube or sizzling like a piece of peat. Not much of a choice. She felt as stuck as a barnacle on a rock.

As if reading her mind, Sage's voice softened. "Look, Isabelle. Your only chance out of this town is to come with me." The cat stretched and rubbed against Sage's leg. "I'm here to take you to your real home, to the place you came from. You have family there, waiting to meet you. But I can't force you to go. You have to decide on your own."

"Family?" Isabelle swallowed hard. Could it be true? "Waiting for me?"

Someone yelled in the distance.

Sage ran to the doorway. "Lanterns," he said. Isabelle followed and peered around his arm. Two yellow lights bobbed near the factory. "They're looking for you along the road. They probably won't check the beach right away. That will give us enough time." He turned to her. "So? What's your decision?"

Now was the time to find out if what she had always believed was true — that she had not been left on that doorstep because she was an unwanted piece of garbage. Finding Nowhere was what she craved with all her heart. Her grandmother's spirit had left for a better place and Isabelle was ready to leave too.

"I'll go with you."

"Then we'd better hurry." He slung his satchel over his back and headed outside. The cat and raven followed.

"How will we get there?" Isabelle called after him. "Which way will we go?"

"We'll go by sea."

The first rays of morning filtered through the clouds,

casting the beach in pale light. The rain had turned to mist, gently coating Isabelle's face as she watched Sage disappear around the rocky bluff. She clutched the pickle jar and ran after him.

"By sea? But where's your boat?" she asked.

Sage pointed to an enormous lump in the sand. "We travel by elephant seal."

Chapter Eleven

HOW TO RIDE AN ELEPHANT SEAL

The elephant seal lay in the sand, snoring — by far the loudest snoring Isabelle had ever heard, even louder than Mama Lu when she'd chugged too much cheese sauce.

"NEPTUNE! THE TIDE IS READY!" Sage shouted. The seal snorted but did not open his eyes. Sage reached into his satchel and pulled out a bright green shirt and matching pants. "Put these on," he told Isabelle.

Isabelle leaned the aquarium against a log. The clothing felt oddly slick and almost slipped from her grasp. "What are these made of?"

"Kelp. They're waterproof. Wear nothing underneath."

"Nothing? Not even . . . ?" She stopped, hoping to avoid the word "underpants."

"Nothing. The wetsuit must form a protective barrier against your skin." He removed his robe. "See, I'm wearing the same thing." He didn't look so mysterious without the robe. The green pants gripped his long skinny legs. They looked like frog legs. "Go on. Hurry up," he said, stuffing his robe into the satchel.

Isabelle wasn't about to change in front of a stranger — especially not one who happened to be a *boy*. With no sign of any lanterns approaching, she ran back to the cabin, where she stripped off her rain slicker and flannel shirt. The fire had burned down to embers, its warmth escaping on the morning breeze. Shivering, Isabelle held up the kelp shirt. It seemed way too small and she couldn't find any buttons or zippers. The hood also looked small, as did the glove on the end of each sleeve. But as she pulled it over her head the weird rubbery fabric stretched to fit perfectly, as if the shirt had been made just for her.

She slid off her boots, socks, canvas pants, and underpants and stepped into the frog pants. They stretched easily. Each leg ended in a bootie that perfectly conformed to her bare feet. She took a few strides around the cabin. The suit was so comfortable that she felt naked. She collected her clothing and ran back to Sage.

"Put your clothes in my satchel. We might need them later." The satchel didn't seem large enough for all her stuff but it must have been made from kelp too, because it stretched to hold everything.

"I'll get the saddle," Sage announced. Then he dragged a contraption from a hiding place behind a log. A tall seat curved gracefully at the back of the saddle and two stirrups hung from the sides. "Now for the tricky part. NEPTUNE!" Sage shoved the seal with both hands but the seal didn't move an inch. "COME ON, YOU FAT THING! I'VE GOT TO PUT THIS ON!" Sage pushed again but the seal only snorted.

Isabelle felt sorry for the seal. It was very rude to yell at someone, even if that someone was an animal. It was especially rude to call someone fat. Isabelle knew this because when Mama Lu and Gertrude got into a fight, they often called each other things like fat, and Mama Lu and Gertrude were the Queens of Rude. But no one else in the boarding-house dared do such a thing. When Mama Lu's old bathrobe no longer fit, Mrs. Limewig had cleverly said, "It must have shrunk." No one would have dared to say, "It's because you eat too much cheese."

"Is that the same sea monster who sneezed the apple onto my lap?" Isabelle asked.

"Yes, but he's not a sea monster. He's an elephant seal. You need to get that straight. And he's a total pain because he's hard of hearing." Sage leaned close to the seal's face and yelled, "ROLL OVER, WILL YOU? WE CAN'T GO ANYWHERE UNTIL YOU PUT THIS ON!"

The seal blinked a few times, then opened his mouth in a gaping drawn-out yawn. When he exhaled, fishy breath blew through Isabelle's hair.

"Watch out," Sage warned as Neptune shifted his weight. "Get out of the way or he'll squish you." Isabelle jumped aside as the seal rolled upright. Sage heaved the saddle onto Neptune's back and fiddled, twisted, cursed, and pulled until he seemed satisfied. He tugged a strap. "Nice and tight, this time. I don't want to fall off again."

"Fall off?" Isabelle shifted nervously. "You mean, into the water?"

"Yep. Neptune didn't hear me calling for help. I had to tread water until Rolo got his attention by pecking him on the head."

"Tread water?"

Sage furrowed his brow. "Why are you looking at me like

that? You mean you don't know how to tread water? Don't tell me you don't know how to swim either."

"No, I don't know how to swim. Why would I know how to swim?" No one in Runny Cove swam. They were wet enough without participating in water sports.

"Oh, that's just great." He folded his arms and frowned. "Did you hear that, Rolo? Not only have I been stuck in this depressing stinkhole of a town for an entire week, but now I've got a passenger who can't swim."

Isabelle didn't like the way he was talking about her, as if she wasn't standing right there. In fact, she was beginning not to like *him*. He was bossy and grumpy, just like Mama Lu and Mr. Supreme — the kind of people she wanted to get away from. "This wasn't my idea," she said curtly. "I didn't ask you to come here and you're being really mean. So what if I don't know how to swim? I bet you don't know how to make an umbrella." Her voice grew shaky. "I bet you don't know how to take care of potato bugs. I bet you don't know . . ."

. . . *what it feels like to have your grandmother die.* She pressed her trembling lips together.

Sage pushed his knotted hair from his face. "Calm down," he said. "It's just that there's a lot at stake. You have no idea."

"I know there's a lot at stake," Isabelle snapped. "I'm in big trouble. I told Mr. Supreme I couldn't work extra hours, and I took Mama Lu's stupid pickle jar. And I don't have a place to live. So don't act like I don't know there's a lot at stake." She turned away and stared across the gray water. Outside the shallows, the waves formed white peaks. "I don't know why you're so grumpy with me, anyway. I didn't make you come here."

"I'm grumpy. It's just the way I am."

Was that supposed to be an apology?

Sage brushed sand off his hands. "Let's just get out of here. NEPTUNE!" The seal had begun to snore again. "NEPTUNE, WAKE UP!"

Isabelle thought that being yelled at was the worst way to be woken up. So she reached out, intending to pet the elephant seal's head.

"STOP!" Sage yelled, pulling her hand away. "You must never touch an elephant seal's nose. Ever. They are very proud of their noses. The bigger the nose, the more powerful the seal. He would be very angry if you touched it."

"I'm . . . I'm sorry," Isabelle said, shaken by the serious look on Sage's face.

"And never insult the nose or make fun of it, either. I made that mistake once. Made a joke about it looking like a dolphin's and Neptune sat on me. I couldn't walk for a week. So no insults. Got it?"

Isabelle nodded. "Be nice to the nose."

Sage moved closer to her. Gold flecks sparkled in his brown eyes. "Before you ride on an elephant seal, you must first pay the seal a compliment. So, instead of saying *Good morning*, or *Hello,* say something like, *That's the biggest nose I've ever seen.* Or, *Thank you for allowing me to be in the presence of such a massive nose.* Go on. Give it a try. Remember to yell or Neptune won't hear you."

Neptune had the strangest nose Isabelle had ever seen and certainly the largest, so she wouldn't be lying. How was it possible that a creature from the sea could understand human language? All those times she had talked to her barnacle about her boring factory job, had it actually been listening?

"Come on, we haven't got all day." Sage gave Isabelle a shove and she stumbled forward.

What a bully! She took a deep breath. "YOU HAVE A LOVELY NOSE!" She wasn't used to yelling and it sent her into a coughing fit.

The elephant seal opened an eye and scrunched his face into a frown.

"No, no," Sage said. "*Lovely* is a word for girl seals. You must compliment the *size* of the nose."

Isabelle cleared her throat. "YOU HAVE THE MOST ENORMOUS NOSE I HAVE EVER SEEN!" Sage motioned for her to continue. "DID I SAY ENORMOUS? I MEANT GARGANTUAN!"

This time, the seal smiled.

Rolo the Raven circled overhead. "Caw, caw."

"Are you certain?" Sage asked the bird. He ran up the beach, so light on his feet that he barely disturbed the sand. He pointed around the rocky outcropping, toward the cove. "Here they come," he said. "Looks like that Mr. Hench has a few men with him. We'd better get going." He whistled.

Eve the cat crawled out from under a log and jumped into the satchel. Rolo continued to caw frantically.

Sage ran back to Neptune. "WE'D BE VERY GRATE-FUL IF YOU'D HAUL YOUR FAT BUTT INTO THE WATER!"

Neptune roared, then raised himself onto his flippers and waddled into the shallows.

"Telling an elephant seal that he has a fat butt is actually a compliment," Sage explained, gathering the satchel. After following Neptune into the water, he grabbed the saddle's horn and pulled himself up. "Come on," he urged.

Isabelle grabbed the pickle jar and waded in. Her legs didn't feel a bit wet or cold. The suit really worked. If all the people of Runny Cove owned kelp suits they'd never feel damp again.

"We can't take that," Sage said, pointing to the aquarium. "It's too big."

"But there's no one here to take care of it," Isabelle pointed out.

"Just drop the barnacle into the water."

She looked down at her boots. The shallows were sandy. "But there aren't any other barnacles here. I don't want it to be all alone."

"Fine." Sage reached in and grabbed the rock upon which the barnacle had attached itself. Then he stuffed the rock into the satchel's side pocket. "The barnacle can live without water for a few days. No problem."

Yellow light flooded the beach. "Thief!" Mr. Hench rounded the rocky corner, swinging his lantern. Two of Mr. Supreme's assistants followed, their long white coats billowing in the morning wind. "You're under arrest!"

Sage held out his hand but Isabelle didn't need his help, not with Mr. Hench closing in. She tossed the pickle jar onto the beach, then leapt behind Sage, swinging her leg over the saddle with the grace of a seasoned jockey.

"Put this around your middle to keep you safe," Sage ordered, handing her a rope. Then he knotted the ends around his own middle. Was she tied to him for safety or had she become his captive? At that moment she didn't care. She just had to get out of there!

"Stop, thief!" Mr. Hench yelled, reaching the water's edge.

"I'm not a thief," Isabelle cried. "Take the stupid pickle jar. I don't want it."

"Hey, where do you think you're going? You've got extra hours to work," one of the assistants called.

"Mr. Supreme will be plenty mad about this," Mr. Hench hollered. "You get back here." He raised his lantern. The light blinded Isabelle. She wrapped her arms around Sage's waist and pressed her face against his back.

"SWIM!" Sage yelled, kicking the seal's sides. "SWIM, YOU BIG-NOSED BRUTE!"

Neptune pushed forward. As soon as he reached deep water, his flabby, rotund body moved as gracefully as a bird in flight. "THAT'S MY SEAL!" Sage yelled as Neptune cut sleekly through the surf.

Isabelle looked over her shoulder. Mr. Hench, who was jumping up and down in a temper tantrum, grew smaller and smaller until he looked as small as a slug on a trampoline.

Rolo the Raven landed on Sage's shoulder. Eve growled unhappily from the satchel, for it is well known that cats do not enjoy sea travel.

"Hold on," Sage said. "Here we go."

Terrified, Isabelle tightened her arms around Sage's waist as Neptune picked up speed. The only home she had ever known disappeared from view, and with it the only people she had ever loved, now doomed to work longer and harder to make Mr. Supreme richer and richer.

"I'll be back," she whispered. "I promise that I'll come back and find a way to help you."

Chapter Twelve
FLOATING IN FOG

A journey usually includes sights to see along the way, like the world's largest ball of twine, a castle made from sand, or maybe even a waxed figure museum. But just beyond Runny Cove, fog rolled in, as thick as porridge. Isabelle narrowed her eyes, straining for a glimpse of anything, but found nothing. Was she drifting across the sea or across the sky? The only way to tell that they were actually moving was from the constant swaying of Neptune's body. But she was on her way and that was all that mattered. She was going to find out where she had come from and in that place a family waited — *her* family.

Isabelle bombarded Sage with questions. "Will I meet my mother and father? Are they tenders too? Do I have any brothers or sisters? Is there going to be a party when I get there? Do I look like my mother? Is she nice? Does my father work in a factory?" She didn't get to ask the most important question of all — *Why was I left on a doorstep?* — because Sage cut her off.

"I can't answer any questions about your family."

"You mean you don't know the answers?"

"Of course I know, but it's really complicated. Besides, someone else wants to tell you."

"Who?"

"You'll find out soon enough. Now stop jabbering."

Isabelle folded her arms and "hmphed" with frustration.

She wasn't jabbering. Asking important questions about one's heritage is totally different from jabbering. You'll find out *soon enough*, he had said. Soon enough seemed like an eternity. She leaned against the saddleback and watched the fog drift past.

With nothing to look at, some might have considered the ride boring. But not Isabelle. She *knew* boring and this was the furthest thing from it. Her frustration quickly turned to excitement, for never in her ten years had she gone anywhere. And the most amazing thing of all, more amazing even than riding on an elephant seal, was that it had stopped raining.

Eve poked her head out of the satchel a few times, then curled up for a nap. Rolo sat on Sage's shoulder, his beak tucked under his black wing. Isabelle wiped sea mist from her face. Neither she nor Sage wore their hoods, since the temperature was quite comfortable.

She decided to risk a non-family question. "Are we almost there?"

He sighed. "No. We've got to travel west for most of the day until we reach the Tangled Islands."

"Is that where Nowhere is? West?"

"West to the Tangled Islands, then north to the Northern Shore. But you might as well start calling Nowhere by its real name — Fortune's Farm."

Grandma Maxine had told Isabelle about farms. There had once been a goat farm and a parsley farm in Sunny Cove. They sounded like pretty places. And the fishermen had often visited a worm farm. "How does Neptune know how to get there? Can he see through all this fog?"

"He can smell the place." Sage turned half around. Mist sparkled at the ends of his long black lashes. How different he looked. There didn't appear to be a speck of mold on him and he didn't wheeze when he breathed like most everyone in Runny Cove. "Neptune's harem lives on the Northern Shore. Last time I counted he had twenty-three wives. You ever smelled a herd of elephant seals?"

Isabelle scratched the itchy patch above her right ear. "Neptune is the first elephant seal I've ever seen. I didn't even know they existed."

"You don't know a lot," Sage said, smirking condescendingly. That may have been the truth. After all, she had never been to school. But did he have to be so rude?

"I'm a fast learner," she said. "Leonard once showed me how to skip rocks and I learned right away. And my grandma taught me how to make a quilt out of old socks."

"You'd better be a fast learner or when you get to Fortune's Farm your head will spin right off." He turned back around. "I'm going to take a nap. It's a long journey so you should take one too." He slumped forward, resting his head on the satchel.

Isabelle couldn't recall ever taking a nap. If she accidentally dozed while standing at the conveyor belt, one of the assistants would wallop her on the head. Besides, if she napped during the sea elephant ride she might miss something. She settled against the saddle and stared into the fog.

Like the ocean's swells, her thoughts rolled and tumbled and her emotions peaked and crested. Going to Nowhere thrilled her. Knowing that she'd never again see her grandmother saddened her. The fact that it had stopped raining amazed her. Riding over deep water scared her. She felt goosebumpy and shivery and sweaty at the same time. So, to ease her mind, she began to compose a little song, which she sang in her head so as not to disturb Sage.

The Elephant Seal Song

Salty water swooshing past,
I might fall off 'cause he's swimming fast.
But I don't care 'cause this is a blast,
on the back of an elephant seal.
What a marvelous way to feel, on the back
of an elephant seal.

I hope Mr. Supreme gets fleas,
and Mama Lu chokes on cheese.
Look at me, doing what I please,
on the back of an elephant seal.
What a marvelous way to feel, on the back
of an elephant seal.

Suddenly she felt lightheaded and woozy. The bread churned in her stomach. She felt worse than she had ever felt, even worse than the time when she'd eaten a bowl of

Mama Lu's "What's that growing in the back of the icebox?" soup. Come the third verse, Isabelle's song took a different tone.

> Up down up down goes the seal,
> down up down up goes my meal.
> But I don't care how bad I feel,
> on the back of an elephant seal.
> What a horrid way to feel, on the back
> of an elephant seal.

Isabelle was seasick. And being seasick is no fun at all.

If you made a list titled "Terrible Things That Are Temporary," seasickness would rank higher than smashing your finger with a hammer, stubbing your toe so hard that the toenail falls off, or accidentally shooting yourself in the bottom with an arrow. It is very common to hear a person who is suffering from seasickness say, "Dear God, please kill me now."

Isabelle felt like a spinning top. She swallowed hard, trying to keep the bile from coming. No use. She leaned over Neptune's flank as far as she could and upchucked into the fog.

"What was that?" Sage asked, rubbing his eyes in confusion as Isabelle upchucked again. "Uh oh. You're not used to this kind of motion." He twisted around as far as he could.

"I feel horrible," she said, wiping her mouth. "Could you take off this rope? It's so tight around my waist. I think it's making things worse."

Sage shook his head. "Way too dangerous. You can't swim, remember?"

Her gut spasmed. "Please. It's pressing too hard." She pulled at the rope but it didn't loosen. She thrashed her legs as nausea washed over her. "Please take it off. I'm going to be sick again."

"Okay, okay. Just don't get sick on me." He untied the rope.

Unfortunately, the rope's release didn't make her feel better. Water sloshed against Neptune's sides as the last bits of bread sloshed in Isabelle's stomach. Uh oh. UH OH!

"Be careful," Sage said. "Don't lean so far . . ."

And that was the last thing Isabelle heard before her head plunged underwater. It felt as if one of Mr. Supreme's assistants had boxed her ears, so shocking was the icy ocean on her face. It took her a moment to realize that she had slipped off the seal. Faint ribbons of light shimmered all around. Salt water stung her eyes as she tried to figure out which way was up. She frantically pumped her legs and arms. Her lungs felt like they might explode. She no longer needed to upchuck — she just needed to breathe!

Something clutched the back of her kelp suit. Up, up, up she moved until she burst onto the surface. She took a huge breath, inhaling seawater as well. She coughed, spitting up the briny stuff.

With a huge groan, Sage pulled Isabelle onto the saddle, this time at the front. "Why did I listen to you?" he snarled. "I should never have untied that rope."

"S . . . s . . . sorry." Though her heart pounded and she still hadn't caught her breath, the icy plunge seemed to have shocked the seasicknesses right out of her. She pushed her dripping hair from her face as Sage secured the rope. Neptune floated patiently.

"Th . . . th . . . thanks," she stammered.

BAROOO!

A horn blasted through the fog. It sounded exactly like the umbrella factory's horn. *Oh no,* Isabelle thought. *Has Neptune gone in the wrong direction? Are we back in Runny Cove?*

BAROOO!

Sage spun around. "It's way too close," he said. "Where is it? Help me look for it."

"Look for what?"

Suddenly, an enormous wall of gray emerged from the fogbank. Taller than any boarding house, faster than any delivery truck, it barreled toward them. Isabelle clutched the saddlehorn. "What is it?"

"Trouble." Sage kicked Neptune. "TURN!" he screamed. "TURN!"

Neptune undulated violently, moving away just in time.

SWOOSH! The enormous structure glided past. Big black letters were painted on its side: MAGNIFICENTLY SUPREME SHIPPING COMPANY. FOR THOSE WITH SUPREME TASTE WHO LIKE TO SHIP THINGS.

As quickly as it had emerged, the ship disappeared into the fog, leaving a wake that rolled beneath the seal. A quieter *barooo* sounded in the distance.

"This place is dangerous," Sage said. "NEPTUNE! AWAY!"

Isabelle wanted to ask more questions, but the seasickness had drained her last bit of strength, as had almost being killed by a ship, losing a grandmother, and running away from Mama Lu.

This time she didn't fight the nap. She leaned against Sage's chest and drifted to sleep.

Chapter Thirteen

THE ISLAND OF
MYSTERIOUS HOLES

A whistle sounded, waking Isabelle from a dreamless sleep. She sat up. *I'm going to be late for work. I can't be late. That would mean extra hours piled on top of extra hours.* She scrambled to her feet, instantly dizzy as blood rushed from her head. *I can't be late. I can't be late.*

As the dizziness cleared, Isabelle found herself standing, not in her vine-covered room, but on a low bluff overlooking a quiet inlet. A small fire crackled inside a ring of rocks. As a delicate rope of smoke arose, so did the memories of yesterday. Grandma Maxine was dead and Runny Cove was far away. Gwen and Leonard were far away too. But a new home and a new family awaited her. She was a tender and only a few people got to be tenders. At least that's what the strange boy had told her. But she still didn't know exactly what that meant. Tenders grow things. That didn't seem like such a big deal. What good was growing mushrooms between your toes? Or lichen on your head? Hadn't he said that someday she might be the last tender in the whole world?

The night had passed but she couldn't remember a bit of it, not even how she had gotten to that bluff. She must have slept hard because a few pebbles had stuck to her cheek. She pulled off her kelp gloves and wiped the pebbles away. Yawning, she turned in a sleepy circle.

Sage was nowhere to be seen, nor was Eve the cat or Rolo

the raven. Isabelle scanned the beach for Neptune but he seemed to be missing as well. Had they left her because she had gotten seasick? *That's a rotten thing to do*, she thought, *to leave a person in the middle of nowhere.* She gasped. Could this be Nowhere? But where were the houses, the factories, and the people? A sense of unease broke through her drowsiness. *What if I'm alone?*

And why is it so quiet?

The answer, she realized, was the lack of rain. One might think this would be a nice change for Isabelle, that she might start kicking out her feet in a happy, rain-free dance, or compose a little song about being dry. But the opposite was true. Imagine waking up one morning to find that you had suddenly gone deaf. That is how it felt to Isabelle. The rain's melody, sometimes delicate, sometimes thunderous, had serenaded her for as long as she could remember. Though it hadn't rained during the journey on Neptune's back, the ocean had provided a constant melody of water and wind. Standing on the bluff, the inlet calm, she could feel the endless silence. Isabelle started humming her little song about Nowhere to fill the emptiness.

That's when a short whistle popped into the air, then faded away. Another whistle followed.

Isabelle stopped humming and spun around. Behind her lay a field of grass and rocks. Behind the field stood a forest of red-barked trees. She waited, holding her breath, watching for movement. A thing that whistles is probably a thing that moves, and she didn't want it sneaking up on her. A boy in a hooded cape, an elephant seal, a ship as big as a factory — what could possibly be next?

Another short whistle shot up from the field, and another. Perhaps the creature was very small — a whistling insect of some sort. Bending close to the ground, to make certain she didn't squish anything, she took a few steps.

Twee, twee.

Then a few more steps.

Twee, twee.

Then she came upon a hole the size of a soup bowl. It wasn't very interesting, as far as holes go. It didn't have any decorative rocks around it or a flag sticking out of it. A hole sat in front of Mr. Supreme's factory with a flag and a plaque that read: GROUND-BREAKING HOLE. ON THIS SACRED GROUND DID MR. SUPREME SENIOR DIG THE FIRST PATCH OF DIRT THAT BECAME THE MAGNIFICENTLY SUPREME UMBRELLA FACTORY, FOR THE EMPLOYMENT OF THE STARVING, DULL-MINDED VILLAGERS OF RUNNY COVE.

Isabelle took a few more steps and found another hole. She stood on tiptoe and scanned the field. Holes lay everywhere, hundreds of them.

"Hey!" a voice called.

Sage emerged from the woods, his satchel flung over his shoulder. He crossed the field, zigzagging around the holes. Eve trotted alongside, a dead mouse swaying from her teeth. Rolo flew overhead. Isabelle forgot all about the whistling, overjoyed to see that she had not been abandoned. Yesterday she hadn't wanted to travel with Sage, but he seemed to hold all the answers to her questions — plus, he had all her stuff inside his satchel.

"Where did you go?" she asked as he approached.

"Just checking things out."

"Is this Nowhere? I mean, is this Fortune's Farm?"

"No. This is one of the Tangled Islands. Neptune dropped us here last night. You were dead asleep." He threw some sticks into the flames then looked to the horizon. "Cloudy. Calm sea. Sun should break through soon."

"Sun?" A wave of excitement washed over Isabelle. Grandma Maxine had often told stories of sunny days spent lying on a picnic blanket or beneath the shade of a tree. But those were stories from long ago, before the rain. "I've never seen the sun."

Sage tossed something into the pan, then stared at her dumbfounded. "Never? Well, that explains why you look like you've been living in a hole and why you're so ugly."

Ugly?

Isabelle turned away, feeling smaller than she had ever felt, her insides shrinking like a salted slug. Mama Lu had called her ugly many times. "Yer an ugly little thing, with that stuff growing in yer hair and those scrawny arms and legs. That's why ya was dumped on the doorstep. Who'd want someone as ugly as you?"

Isabelle had tried not to take Mama Lu's comments to heart. After all, Mama Lu had never said anything nice about anybody. But when Sage, the boy who had rescued her, called her ugly, it hurt like a punch in the gut. Isabelle wanted to hurt him right back.

"What do you know, anyway?" she mumbled. "You don't look so good. Your hair is a mess. It looks like you never even brush it."

"I don't," he said. "That's the point. I *want* to look this way. You couldn't possibly want to look *that* way, with your skin all puckered and see-through. It looks like the rain washed all the color right off of you."

"Maybe I do want to look this way." She folded her arms and glared at him. "Anyway, you're just jealous because I'm a tender and you're not." She didn't yet know the significance of this statement but from the stunned look on his face, she knew that she had hurt his feelings. "So there!"

Isabelle turned her back to him, angered by his rudeness and ashamed of her own. She wiped her stuffy nose on her sleeve.

"You're not crying are you?" He sighed with exasperation. "Look, Isabelle, I didn't mean to say it like that. Ugly's not the right word. It's just that you look so . . . unhealthy. And you don't look anything like a tender. You'll be surprised when you get to Fortune's Farm."

"You mean my mother and father don't look like me?"

He scowled. "I told you I can't answer any questions about your family. You'll just have to wait."

An unfamiliar scent drifted up Isabelle's nostrils. Sage crouched next to the fire and poked at the sizzling contents of the pan with a stick. Isabelle's stomach growled loudly. "Come on. You'll like this," he said.

She sat beside him and eagerly ate all that she was given —

eight slices of bacon, a large chunk of smoked salmon, and a mug of peppermint tea — foods that she had never tasted before. The surface of the tea glistened with bacon grease but that didn't bother her one bit. Eve the cat happily chewed on a mouse tail, growling when Rolo got too close. Sage tossed a piece of bacon rind to the raven. Isabelle didn't say a word until she had finished the last bite of her meal. Feeling full was as unfamiliar to her as rainless silence. And it felt good. Really good.

She drained her mug. "How far away is the Northern Shore?"

"Hopefully we'll land by dinner, if that good-for-nothing seal would hurry and finish hunting." Sage scraped the pan clean, then stuffed it into his satchel.

As much as she wanted to get to Fortune's Farm, Isabelle wasn't looking forward to riding Neptune again. All that rocking to and fro might upset her lovely breakfast. She stretched her legs and leaned back, spreading her fingers in the soft grass. The fog had lifted above the horizon, revealing scattered islands sprinkled with trees and edged with rugged cliffs. Back home, Isabelle had often gazed at the cove's horizon, but never had there been anything to see. *Each of those islands is a different place,* she thought. *A different world I know nothing about.*

"Ouch!" She pulled her hand out of the grass. A droplet of blood dripped from her pinkie. "Something bit me." She put her finger to her mouth.

Sage pointed. "There's the villain."

Chapter Fourteen
A NEW FRIEND

Isabelle turned to find a pair of black eyes staring up at her. Attached to the black eyes was a body about the same size as Eve's, only covered in brown fur, with a shorter, thicker tail. The "villain" sat on its hind legs, exposing a belly of yellow fur. The nails on its little paws were long and two big front teeth rested on its lower lip. It wiggled its black nose at her and blinked. Then it whistled and darted into the field, disappearing down a hole.

"What was that?" Isabelle asked, still sucking on her finger.

"A yellow-bellied marmot. You gotta watch out for them. They're little devils. I don't know what they're doing out here on this island. They usually live inland. At the rate they reproduce, there soon won't be enough food for all of them."

"Why'd it bite me?"

"Just protecting its territory. If you get too close to its den, it'll hit you right in the head with a rock. Believe me. I know." He looked out over the inlet. "Neptune better not forget to come back. If he forgets me one more time, I'm getting myself a new seal."

Isabelle examined her finger. The bite wasn't deep and it stopped bleeding right away. As Sage continued packing things into his satchel, she remembered something. "Do you think we should put my barnacle into some water?" she asked.

"I already did. I found the perfect new home for it." He motioned for her to follow.

They climbed down the bluff. Isabelle's kelp booties gripped the flat black stones that covered the beach. At the water's edge she and Sage knelt beside a tide pool thick with barnacles. Little white feathers fanned the water as the barnacles fed. Or maybe they were talking to each other. Maybe they were one big family.

"There it is," Sage said.

Sure enough, Isabelle's little barnacle sat on its rock, right in the center of the tide pool, also fanning the water. Isabelle smiled. "It's the perfect place," she said, surprised by Sage's thoughtfulness. "Thank you."

He lowered his head and mumbled, "No big deal."

A roar filled the air. "Finally," Sage said, leaping to his feet. "WHERE HAVE YOU BEEN?" The seal hauled himself out of the shallows and a full-blown argument ensued, with Sage hollering and shaking his fists, and the seal roaring and whacking Sage with his flippers.

Isabelle took a long, last look at her barnacle. "I hope you'll be happy here," she whispered. She felt proud and victorious, having saved something from Mama Lu's stomping feet. Too bad she hadn't been able to save the others. *Two of us escaped. Take that, Mama Lu!*

Something hit the back of Isabelle's arm.

A marmot sat on a log, a stone's throw away. It wiggled its black nose and blinked. "Hey," Isabelle said, rubbing her arm. Another marmot popped out from behind the log and joined its friend. They greeted one another by touching noses. Then they balanced on their hind legs and stared at Isabelle.

"Go on. Shoo."

They didn't shoo. One picked up a rock and threw it at her.

"Ouch!" She rubbed her shoulder. "Stop doing that." Was she standing near one of their holes? No. But still, they stared. "What do you want?"

The two marmots jumped off the log and scampered up the beach to where a giant tree had fallen. They climbed up the fallen tree's trunk and chirped, a softer, friendlier sound than the whistle. They stared at her, chirped, stared, chirped — clearly telling her something. Sage was busy with the saddle, so with a shrug, Isabelle approached the tree, shielding her face with her hands in case they took aim again.

Dozens of empty broken crates lay hidden behind the fallen tree. Each had a label that read: HANDLE WITH CARE. CONTAINS LIVE LABORATORY ANIMALS. SPECIES: YELLOW-BELLIED MARMOT.

The marmots ran along the trunk, then lay on their bellies and hung their heads over a branch. A furry marmot bottom poked out from under the branch. The creature's little legs kicked frantically but to no avail — it was stuck. The two marmots chirped softly to their trapped friend.

"Poor little thing," Isabelle said as the legs continued to kick. "I'll help you." She crouched next to the wiggling bottom and pulled at the branch with all her might until it snapped off. Branch in hand, she tumbled backwards.

The marmot waddled out and scratched its head with its leg. Except for a small cut above its right eye, it looked unhurt.

Isabelle was about to sit up when the freed marmot climbed onto her chest and sat itself down as if it meant to stay awhile. It leaned forward and peered into her eyes. Isabelle held her breath. Was it going to bite her nose with its buck teeth? It leaned closer but rather than biting her, it pressed its wet nose against hers. She giggled as its fur brushed her face. It nosed her again. Then the freed marmot greeted its friends. They touched noses, chirped, and scurried around one another. It was the happiest dance Isabelle had ever seen.

"Isabelle!" Sage called. "Time to go!"

She scrambled to her feet and ran back down the beach.

"Where were you?"

"I was over there," she said, pointing to the distant tree.

Sage frowned and pointed at her feet. "And what are you doing with that?"

The rescued marmot had followed Isabelle down the beach and had wedged itself between her kelp booties.

"It was stuck. I helped it."

"Oh." Sage's expression softened for a moment. Then he turned serious again. "We need to catch the tide."

"Goodbye," Isabelle said, waving down to the marmot. Then she ran over and greeted the glistening seal. "YOUR NOSE IS LOOKING EXTREMELY LOVELY . . . I MEAN, EXTREMELY BULBOUS THIS MORNING."

Neptune nodded and tilted his head so Isabelle could scratch his chin. The marmot whistled and threw a rock at Neptune, who didn't even notice — like a grain of rice bouncing off a truck.

"COME ON, LET'S GO!" Sage pushed Neptune's rump.

Neptune rose up on his flippers and made his way into the shallows. Sage tucked Eve into the satchel and secured it to the saddle's horn. Then he climbed on board. Rolo watched from the branch of a red-barked tree. The marmot scurried across the wet sand and sat on Isabelle's foot.

"I've got to go," she told the furry creature.

"Hurry up," Sage urged. "We need to make the Northern Shore by nightfall."

Isabelle tried to gently push the marmot off her foot but it flattened its body and chirped softly. "I think it wants to go with me." She picked it up and held it at arm's length, still unsure of those teeth. "Do you want to go with us?"

"No way," Sage said. "We don't have room for another passenger. There's no place to put it."

The marmot wiggled its bottom, then climbed up Isabelle's arm and onto her shoulder, where it squirmed its way down the back of her kelp shirt. Its little claws tickled but didn't prick her skin. The shirt stretched as the marmot turned itself around and popped its head back out through the neck hole. Its furry belly felt warm against her back. It sniffed her earlobe. Isabelle giggled. "I don't think I have a choice."

Sage grumbled to himself. "Fine. But it better not have fleas."

Isabelle settled behind Sage. She helped tie the rope around her middle. The marmot made little wheezy sounds as it breathed in her ear. "Do marmots get seasick?" she asked.

"Probably, knowing my luck." Sage gave Neptune a kick. The seal pushed itself into the deep water.

"What should I feed it if it gets hungry?" Isabelle asked, scratching the marmot's head.

"I don't know." Sage checked the rope again. "By the way, it's a she."

"A she?"

"Yes. She's a girl marmot."

"Oh, how nice."

Rolo flew overhead as Neptune wove between rocky reefs. Back on the island, a chorus of marmot chirps filled the air. Isabelle sensed it was a song of farewell, but if the marmot felt sad about leaving, she didn't show it. She nestled her face against Isabelle's neck and fell asleep.

Isabelle supposed that a barnacle-filled tide pool was a great place for her barnacle to live. But an overpopulated island was a horrible place for a marmot, just as a boarding-house run by Mama Lu in a town where it never stopped raining was a horrible place for a person. She and her new friend were not so different, each looking for a better home. Perhaps, before falling asleep, the marmot had made the same promise that Isabelle had made — to return one day and help her friends.

Maybe, just maybe, they would both fulfill their promises.

Chapter Fifteen

GREAT-UNCLE WALNUT

Once they reached the outer edge of the Tangled Islands, the sea lay wide and calm. Isabelle tried to get comfortable, though getting comfortable in a saddle with a drooling marmot stuck to one's back is not an easy feat.

The journey to the Northern Shore took most of the day. Sage continued to withhold information. Pestering and poking didn't work on him. "You'll have to wait," he grumbled.

"I don't want to wait," Isabelle said. "I just want to know more about being a tender."

"If you poke me one more time, I'll turn this seal around and then you'll never know."

"Fine! I'll wait."

Isabelle had spent her whole life waiting — for the sun to shine, for Mama Lu to make something decent to eat, for the next box to wind its way to her station. "Waiting is a waste of time," Grandma Maxine had told her. "Because in the end what you'll probably get is one big fat disappointment and then what do you have to show for all that waiting? You should be doing, not waiting."

But what was there to "do" on the back of a seal other than ask questions? And as hard as she tried, no new songs popped into her head. What if, at the end of this journey, being a tender turned out to be one big fat disappointment? What would she do? Where would she go?

It was late afternoon when a cacophony of barking woke her from a troubled and slightly nauseated nap. Neptune had stopped swimming and the water around them churned and frothed. A sharp stench shot up her nostrils. The marmot tightened her grip around Isabelle's neck. "What's going on?" Isabelle asked.

"It's Neptune's harem," Sage explained.

In every direction seals poked their heads from the water, blinking large brown eyes and snorting through flared nostrils. Their noses weren't pendulous like Neptune's. Here and there smaller heads poked up — Neptune's children. Their gray shapes darted beneath and above the water line, somersaulting and rolling as gracefully as waves. Neptune surveyed the welcome party with a proud smile. *How nice*, Isabelle thought, *to have such a large family.*

"TO THE SHORE!" Sage called, kicking Neptune urgently.

The Northern Shore stretched out before them — speckled beach, clay banks, and fir trees as far as the eye could see. Rolo took flight, disappearing over the treetops. The marmot crawled from the kelp shirt and stood on Isabelle's shoulders, draping her body over Isabelle's head for a better view. Neptune caught the face of a wave and slid onto the beach.

As soon as the seal came to a complete stop, Isabelle scrambled off his back and carefully meandered between the other seals that mingled at the water's edge. The marmot scampered up the beach, squatting to pee beside a log. *Thank goodness she didn't do that in my shirt*, Isabelle thought.

Sage removed the saddle and flung it onto the beach. He patted the seal's head. "GOOD JOB, NEPTUNE!" The seal nodded, then nose-butted Sage's legs. Sage shoved back. Neptune followed with a flipper swat, Sage followed with a slap, until the two were playfully punching each other like brothers. The battle ended when Neptune pinned Sage to the ground. "OKAY, OKAY! I GIVE UP!"

Sage scrambled to his feet. "Best say goodbye," he told Isabelle.

"Neptune's not coming with us?"

"Of course not. Have you ever heard of an elephant seal climbing a mountain?"

Isabelle didn't know whether seals climbed mountains or not, but she didn't say so. She'd never seen a mountain but she didn't mention that either. Sage would just tell her, again, that she didn't know anything.

Isabelle knelt in front of Neptune's thick head and looked into his dark eyes. So much had happened since that night on the beach when she had thought he was a sea monster. "THANK YOU FOR THE RIDE! AND THANKS FOR THE APPLE!"

Neptune roared softly, his fishy breath warming Isabelle's face. Then he pulled himself back into the depths. His family followed, churning the water like porridge bubbling in a pot.

"Will we see him again?" Isabelle asked. Despite how bad he smelled and how seasick she got when she rode on him, she had come to like the big guy.

"I can't think why you'd ever see him again. You'll be living on Fortune's Farm from now on. No need for you to travel by sea."

"But what about when I go back to Runny Cove? Will Neptune take me?"

Sage opened the satchel, freeing Eve the cat, who shook herself, then scampered off. "Go back? Why would you ever go back to that stink hole?"

"To get Gwen. She's an orphan and my best friend. She could come and live on the farm with me."

Sage straightened his long body and stared down at Isabelle. "I'd get that idea out of my head if I were you. Things don't work that way." Before she could say anything, he handed the satchel to her, then hefted the saddle over his shoulder. "Don't start in with the questions. Let's just go."

How could he expect her not to ask questions? That was as ridiculous as expecting a slug not to ooze a trail of slime. Or expecting Mama Lu to bake a birthday cake for someone other than herself. Isabelle tightened her grip on the satchel as she followed Sage up the beach. "Then who is going to answer my questions? That's what I'd like to know, because I'm still very confused."

"And I'm *very tired.* I found you, didn't I? I'm taking you to Fortune's Farm, aren't I? All I ask is that you stop asking questions that I'm not supposed to answer. You'll find out soon enough."

"Fine!"

The late afternoon sky, though cloud-covered, shone brighter than Isabelle was used to. She had taken to squinting since leaving Runny Cove and her cheeks ached because of it.

They walked through a grove of pine trees, passing over a forest floor of dappled shadows and moss. Eve strutted proudly, her tail sticking straight up. While the cat walked a straight, determined path, the marmot zipped up and down, over and under, occasionally stopping to sit on her hind legs and look around.

Isabelle grumbled to herself. She wanted to tell Sage that he was rude, and rotten, and mean for not answering her questions. But each time a question rolled onto her tongue, she clamped her lips tight to keep it from escaping. She'd know *soon enough.*

"Here we are," Sage announced.

They stepped out of the forest and into a little meadow where a wooden caravan sat. It resembled a yellow house on wheels, with windows on the side and a door in back. A creek meandered through the meadow, sparkling as it trickled past.

"What are those?" Isabelle asked, stopping in her tracks.

Two creatures stood beside the creek, their heads bowed as they drank water.

"Don't tell me you've never seen oxen before," Sage said, dumping the saddle in the grass.

Okay. I won't tell you.

Sage knocked on the caravan's door. "I'm back." He

128

opened the door and stuck his head in. Eve leapt into the caravan. Sage cupped his hands over his mouth and yelled, "Walnut! Where are you?" The oxen raised their horned heads but did not offer an answer.

"Who's Walnut?" Isabelle asked, dropping the heavy satchel.

"He's going to drive us to Fortune's Farm." Sage put his hands on his hips and walked in a slow circle, surveying the surroundings. "He's probably fallen asleep again. I just have to look carefully . . . there he is." Sage walked over to a mound of shrubbery. "Yep, that's him."

A shrub was going to drive them to Fortune's Farm? Isabelle held back the question, knowing full well that Sage's response would be, "Don't tell me you've never seen a shrub that can drive." The marmot tapped on Isabelle's foot to be picked up, then draped herself over Isabelle's head to get a better view. Certainly, that marmot was the heaviest and wheeziest hat that Isabelle had ever worn.

"He's under here somewhere," Sage said. "He's a tender, just like you."

Isabelle gasped. "You mean, I'm going to turn into a shrub?"

"No." Sage pushed back the shrub's branches, snapping some off in the process, until a curled-up old man came into view. "This always happens when he falls asleep. When he touches things they grow extra-fast. If he stays in one place for too long, whatever he's sitting on or lying on starts to grow. Hey, Walnut. Wake up."

The old man yawned. He scratched the bald spot at the top of his head. His long white hair grew in a ridge above his ears and hung past his shoulders. "Where am I?" he asked, spitting out a leaf.

"The Northern Shore," Sage replied. "You fell asleep."

"Oh. Why, hello, Sage." He sat up and his wrinkled face folded into a smile. He had a gentle face that reminded Isabelle of the twins, Boris and Bert. But unlike the twins, the Walnut fellow had a full set of teeth.

Sage held out his hand and helped Walnut to his feet. "I've just returned from Runny Cove," Sage told him.

"What's that you say?" Walnut pushed back his hair and pulled a fern out of his ear, roots and all. "*Fernicus Splendiferous*," he mumbled, examining the plant. "Native only to the Northern Shore. Prefers moist soil, filtered light and, so it would seem, ear cavities."

Sage rolled his eyes. "Walnut, I've brought the tender."

"Oh?" Walnut stuffed the fern into his pocket and pulled another fern from his other ear. "Say again?"

"The tender. The one we've been looking for."

"Why yes, of course. Where is he?"

"Behind you."

The old man pulled a pair of glasses from the pocket of his plaid jacket and perched them on the ridge of his nose. Then he turned and looked at the front of Isabelle, then walked around to her back, then back to her front again. Isabelle stood very still. She had been inspected many times before. Mr. Supreme's assistants always inspected the workers to make certain no one tried to sneak an umbrella out of the factory, and Mama Lu inspected her tenants for hitch-hiking slugs.

Walnut furrowed his brow and shook his head. "I don't think this is a boy, Sage. I think it's a girl."

Sage rolled his eyes again.

Was Walnut the person who would answer all of her questions? It didn't seem likely, if he had been expecting a boy. He stood about the same height as Isabelle so when he leaned close they were nose to nose. He blinked eyes as green as moss. "She doesn't look anything like a Fortune. Are you certain?"

"She made the Love Apple seed sprout. She's got it with her."

Walnut pushed his glasses further up his nose. "But whatever is the matter with her head? She's got another set of eyes right at the top of her head. Is she . . . deformed?"

Isabelle pushed the marmot onto her shoulder. "It's my marmot," she explained.

Walnut scratched his nose with a dirt-stained fingernail and peered at the furry creature. "Yellow-bellied *Marmoticus Terriblus*, a rock-throwing rodent native to the mountainous regions of the north. Impressive frontal fangs." Then he turned his attention back to Isabelle. "You don't look very healthy. Are you dying?"

"I don't think so." Isabelle stifled a cough.

"It's just that you're so pale and thin. You look like you've been living in a hole."

"I've been living at Mama Lu's Boardinghouse." The cough overtook her and she turned away, her lungs rattling with each breath.

"Living in Runny Cove *is* like living in a hole," Sage told Walnut. "There's no sun."

"No sun?" Walnut gasped. "How can a tender live without sun? Well, all that will soon change. She'll soak up the sun like a banana tree. What's this?" He peeled a piece of lichen from Isabelle's hair. *"Lichen Itchycus."* He smiled. "How wonderful. I wasn't able to grow Lichen Itchycus until after my twentieth birthday. What else can you grow?"

Isabelle cleared her throat. "Mushrooms. But only after I've been walking in the mud and my socks get all wet."

"Between your toes?"

"Yes."

"Delightful! *Fungus Amongus,* a toe-loving mushroom with culinary aspirations. I have known a few people who were squeamish about eating toe mushrooms but I can assure you that the soup is to die for."

"Now do you believe me?" Sage asked. "She's the missing tender."

"Indeed." The old man clapped his hands. "Indeed, indeed, indeed." Then he grabbed Isabelle's hand and shook it. "Welcome. My name is Walnuticus Bartholomew Fortune, but you can call me Great-Uncle Walnut."

"Great-uncle?" Isabelle's entire body stiffened. This was it. The *it* she had dreamed about. "Really? You are my great-uncle?"

"None other." He let go of her hand and freed a bit of shrubbery from his sleeve. "And what might your name be?"

"Isabelle."

Walnut frowned. "Isabelle? That's not much of a name, is it? Not the sort of family name we usually have. Would you be amenable to changing it, say perhaps to Floribundy, or Violabombola?"

Isabelle shrugged. "I've always been Isabelle."

"We should get going," Sage interrupted. "I'll hitch the oxen." He strode over to the creek.

Walnut pointed the bit of shrubbery at Isabelle. "What about Horticulturina? She was your great-great-great-great-grandmother. Truly one of the finest tenders the world has ever known. Her spit could quench a plant's thirst for months at a time — most convenient during a drought. But Isabelle? Who could possibly have chosen such a plain name as Isabelle?"

Isabelle didn't want to hurt her great-uncle's feelings, having just met him. But her Grandma Maxine had chosen the name and it had always seemed like a fine name. And the names Uncle Walnut had mentioned were long and difficult to pronounce.

"Are you really my great-uncle?"

"Indeed. Brother to your grandfather."

"I have a grandfather?" Her voice rose excitedly. It was all coming true, just as she had hoped. She had a family.

Walnut cleared a few more branches from his clothing. "What about Petuniarium? That was my mother's name.

Or Larkspuria? That was the name of my first love." He sighed, then snapped his fingers. "Oh, I know. Why not change your name to Vanillabeanly since you are so pale. I think that suits you. Vanillabeanly Fortune."

Luckily, Isabelle didn't have to tell her great-uncle that she thought all those names were a bit weird, because Rolo the raven swooped from the sky, filling the meadow with his cries.

Sage, who had been leading the oxen toward the caravan, stopped and craned his neck. "Where?" he called out.

The raven replied, circling frantically.

Sage grabbed the oxen by their collars. "We must leave immediately," he cried. "Did you hear me, Walnut? Right now."

Walnut removed his glasses and slid them back into his jacket pocket. "Dear boy, why are you in such a hurry? This is a family reunion. Surely we have time for a cup of tea?"

"No, we don't. According to Rolo, we've got trouble."

Chapter Sixteen
TROUBLE ON THE TRAIL

Trouble? What kind of trouble?" Isabelle asked. But neither Walnut nor Sage answered, for a flurry of activity had erupted. Sage hitched the oxen while Great-Uncle Walnut ran around the caravan, gathering up personal belongings. He threw Sage's satchel and the saddle into the back, patted Eve on the head, then bolted the door. Then he hoisted himself onto the driver's bench.

"Come on, Isabelle," he called, holding out a hand.

Isabelle grabbed the marmot and climbed onto the cushioned bench. Walnut flicked the reins and the oxen began to pull the caravan from the meadow. "Where's Sage?" Isabelle asked.

"Don't worry about him," Walnut said. "He ran ahead to look for danger. It's his job to protect the tenders." He flicked the reins again but the oxen appeared to have only one speed — lumbering.

"Protect us from what?"

"I don't wish to worry you, dear, but we must keep our voices quiet. There are people who would like to get rid of us tenders."

Isabelle shivered. "Get rid of?"

"Kill us, to put it bluntly."

"Kill?" Isabelle nearly shrieked the word.

"There are others who would like to kidnap us and imprison us. Some would torture us for our secrets, even enslave us. That's why we must always keep the location of our farm a secret. But I do not wish to worry you." Not a twinkle to be found in his eyes, nor a smile hidden at the corners of his mouth. He was dead serious.

Why would Sage want to be a tender if it meant getting kidnapped, tortured, or killed? After all her waiting, being killed would be far worse than being disappointed. At least no one in Runny Cove wanted to kill her!

"But why would someone want to kill me?" The marmot squeezed onto the bench, curling into a nap between the two tenders. "Is it because I grew things inside? Mama Lu said I wasn't supposed to grow things inside her house. She got really mad. But I didn't do it on purpose."

"Ah, I see that Sage hasn't told you much." Walnut kept his voice low. "I asked him not to. Thought it best to come from a family member." He leaned in close. "What we tenders do is grow magic."

"Magic? But magic's not real."

"'Course it's real. As real as this sapling." The back of the driver's bench, against which Walnut leaned, had sprouted. He pulled out the sapling and tossed it onto the trail. "You do know what magic is, don't you?"

"Magic's when you close your eyes, make a wish, and it comes true."

"No, that's coincidence."

"Magic's when a princess kisses a frog and it turns into a prince."

"No, that's evolution."

 137

Isabelle scratched her neck. "Well, then, what is magic?"

"A gift, dear Isabelle. A gift from long, long ago." He flicked the reins again. The oxen snorted. "Tenders are the only people in the entire world who can grow magical ingredients."

"What do you mean, exactly, by magical ingredients?"

Walnut peered around the edge of the caravan, then leaned in close. "If someone wants to cast a magical spell, that person needs certain ingredients. Do you see? Only a tender can grow those ingredients."

"Like Love Apples?"

"Exactly. Now, we must be quiet. Keep your eyes peeled for Rolo. He will warn us if danger lies in wait."

Isabelle tried to be quiet but a sneeze forced its way out.

"*Pneumonia Stubbornia*, which is Latin for a cold that won't go away," Walnut said, shaking his head. "Poor Isabelle. I'll give you some medicine for that as soon as we get to the farm." Then he asked, a bit shyly, "This Mama Lu you mentioned. Is she married?"

"She used to be."

"I've been searching for a wife for some time. Do you think . . ."

"No!" Isabelle stuck out her tongue. "She's horrid and rotten and mean."

Walnut sighed. "I'm sorry to hear that."

Late afternoon turned to dusk, as it typically does. The trail followed alongside a river, climbing steadily into the mountains. In places the river flowed deep and smooth. In other places it rushed by, churning around rocks and stumps. Beyond the river stood a forest with trees taller than the boarding houses that lined Boggy Lane. They grew in clusters, reaching out to one another with arched branches like friends holding hands.

Who were these horrible people who wanted to hurt tenders? Isabelle scanned the sky for signs of the raven. She watched for Sage at each bend in the trail, hoping he would be waiting to say that all was well. The sky darkened and for a moment, she lost sight of the trail. Her heart began to beat wildly as the oxen slowed even more. Then, she nearly fell off the bench. "What's that?"

"What?" Walnut, who had nodded off, sat up straight.

"That!"

He cleared some soil from his ear. "Bat? Did you say bat? Which species? *Vampiria* or *Fruitola*?"

"No. I said, *What's that?*" Isabelle pointed at the ridge of light above the trees.

"That is a moonrise, of course." Walnut took a knit hat from his coat pocket and pulled it over his bald spot.

The moon peeked over the trees, quickly gliding into full view. Hanging alone in the sky, it reminded Isabelle of the lightbulb in her bedroom, only the moon didn't have to abide by Mama Lu's eight o'clock shutoff rule. And it was much, much bigger. "How does it do that?" she asked. "How does it make so much light?"

Uncle Walnut cleared his throat. "Yes, well, er . . . You see . . ." He cleared his throat again. "A very complicated system of circuits and wiring but the details have escaped me at the moment. Nothing to do with magic, I know that much."

"It's beautiful," Isabelle said with a sigh, momentarily forgetting that danger might await them around the next corner. Her head filled with music as a song begged to be born. So many things rhymed with moon she could write a dozen songs.

Walnut yawned and stretched his legs, as did the marmot. The reins slipped from his hands and his chin dropped as he fell back to sleep. The oxen seemed to know where to go without his help, plodding along the steep trail at an even pace. Isabelle still couldn't believe she was sitting next to a member of her family. She reached out to touch her great-uncle's wrinkled hand, but drew back, reminded of Grandma Maxine's hands. She turned away, trying to squeeze the image of the empty bed from her mind.

Moon, June, tune, spoon, monsoon . . .

The caravan tilted as the trail took a sharp turn. The oxen stopped and snorted a greeting as Sage ran toward them. He reached up and grabbed the slack reins. "We've got to get off the trail," he whispered. Then he pulled the oxen into a small clearing. "Walnut, wake up."

The old man's head lolled to the side.

Sage climbed onto the seat and pulled a newly sprouted fern from Walnut's ear. "Wake up," he repeated.

"What's that?" Walnut opened his eyes.

"We've got company," Sage said.

While the marmot dozed on the bench, Isabelle and Walnut followed Sage down the trail and crouched behind a large boulder. An odd sort of contraption sat up ahead. The words SUPREME GYROCOPTERS — FOR THOSE WITH SUPREME TASTE WHO PREFER TO SOAR were painted on its side. Two men sat next to the contraption, eating sandwiches. They wore long white coats, just like the assistants back in the umbrella factory. White goggles perched on their heads. One of them sported a bulbous wart on his nose. "I say we wait until morning, then we see where this trail goes," he said.

"Waste of time if you ask me," said the other one, who sported a unibrow. "Why would somebody keep a farm up in these mountains? There ain't no farms up here. I say we're looking in the wrong place."

"That's the point, stupid," said Wart Nose. "The farm's hidden somewhere where you wouldn't think to find a farm. We got our orders. Mr. Supreme says we can't leave 'til we search the entire area."

Was Mr. Supreme looking for Fortune's Farm?

The marmot scampered onto Isabelle's lap, a rock held firmly in her paw. The men stuffed their cheeks with sandwiches.

"That gyrocopter is blocking the trail," Sage whispered to Walnut. "And the old mountain pass is too dangerous for the oxen."

Walnut took his glasses from his pocket and slid them onto his nose. "I wholeheartedly agree." He reached into another pocket and pulled out a paper packet. "I don't see another way. Do you?"

Sage glanced at the packet. "Let's do it."

"Do what?" Isabelle asked, hugging the marmot to her chest.

"Stay here," Walnut told her. "This is far too dangerous for an untrained tender." He patted Isabelle's back, then walked around the boulder and onto the trail, with Sage at his heels. "Good evening, gentlemen."

The two men jumped to their feet. "What's this?" Wart Nose asked. "Where'd you come from?"

"Wondering the same thing about you," Sage said.

"Stop right there," ordered Unibrow, pulling something shiny from his pocket and pointing it at Sage.

Chapter Seventeen

THE SOLEMN PROMISE

Keep quiet," Sage called out to Isabelle. "And stay down. He's got a gun."

The only gun Isabelle had ever seen was the one Mr. Hench used to kill factory rats. One bullet was all it took to send a rat soaring across a room, dead. She peered around the boulder. *Don't kill Sage,* she wanted to yell. *He's not a tender.* But instinct told her to mind Sage and keep quiet.

Unibrow pointed the gun at Walnut, then back at Sage. "You two wouldn't happen to know anything about a place called Fortune's Farm, would you?"

Isabelle clutched the marmot tighter. How could Mr. Supreme know about Fortune's Farm? It was supposed to be secret.

With his teeth, Walnut ripped open the packet, then poured something into his hand.

"Hey, what are you doing?" Wart Nose asked. "What do you got there?"

"They're just little plants," Walnut replied, holding out his hand. Green shoots slithered between his fingers. In an instant, the shoots shot out like arrows and coiled around Unibrow's feet and torso, growing so quickly that before he could scream, he was ensnared in a tangled mass of thick vines. Unibrow made not a sound as he completely disappeared from view.

"What the . . . ?" Wart Nose scrambled for the gyrocopter. The marmot climbed onto the boulder and hurled her rock, which hit Wart Nose in the back of the head. "AHHH!" Wart Nose cried. As Walnut poured more seeds into his palm, Rolo flew from a tree and dropped another rock onto Wart Nose's head. More shoots flew through the air and entangled Wart Nose before he could climb into the gyrocopter. With an eerie *whoosh* they completely encased him and he disappeared from sight.

Isabelle ran out from behind the boulder. She circled the large green lump that had once been Mr. Supreme's uni-browed assistant. "Was that magic?" she asked.

"Indeed," Walnut replied, folding the seed packet and re-turning it to his pocket. "My tending skills make things grow extra fast. It's mostly annoying but sometimes it comes in handy."

Sage rolled the green lump to the side of the trail.

"Is he dead?" The question made Isabelle queasy.

"Oh, no. If I had wanted to kill him I would have used the seeds from the Piranha Plant." Walnut wiped his hands on his coat. "I used Vice Vines, aptly named for their vice-like grip. They are happiest when they have something, or in this case, *someone*, to squeeze. Vice Vines, however, have very short attention spans and quickly grow bored with squeezing."

"Then we'd better get going," Sage said, rolling the sec-ond lump to the side of the road. "There's no telling how many more of Supreme's goons are out here. I'll go get the caravan." He ran off.

"Isabelle," Walnut said, placing a hand gently on her shoulder. "We tenders do not normally use magic for violent purposes. But there are times when it is necessary." He straightened his hat. "But an untrained tender should never use Vice Vines because they can backfire. I learned that the hard way and it was six whole months before I returned to my normal shape."

Isabelle imagined flinging Vice Vines at Mama Lu. The tenants would cheer as the blue bathrobe and fleshy face disappeared, until all that stuck out was a pair of enormous fuzzy slippers.

Under Sage's guidance, the oxen pushed the gyrocopter off the trail and into the rushing river. The travelers climbed onto the caravan's bench where Sage took the reins, with Isabelle and Walnut on either side. The marmot curled up on Isabelle's lap. "I think she threw that rock to protect you," Isabelle told Sage.

"I think you're right." Sage patted the marmot's head.

"*Marmoticus Terriblus* never miss their target," Walnut said.

Isabelle stretched her kelp shirt over the marmot's body, enclosing her little friend in a warm cocoon. "I'm going to name her Rocky."

Isabelle's eyelids began to droop. She didn't have the energy to ask all the new questions that had lined up in her mind. Her neck felt rubbery and her head fell forward a few times. She closed her eyes, vaguely aware that the oxen had pulled off the trail. She dozed for a while, until Walnut took her hand. "Wake up, Isabelle."

A sheer rock wall towered before them, so tall that Isabelle could not see where it ended. "Isabelle," Walnut said, "I'd like you to go and touch the side of that mountain."

Sage frowned. "Not yet. She has to make the promise."

"I don't think that's necessary. She can do that later."

"She *must* make the promise."

"Oh, very well." Walnut pulled a piece of lichen from Isabelle's hair. "Isabelle, all Fortunes must make a solemn promise to never reveal the whereabouts of Fortune's Farm. Are you willing to do this?"

She rubbed her sleepy eyes. "You mean I can't tell anyone? Not even Gwen?"

"No one. You must also promise never to take anything from Fortune's Farm without the Head Tender's permission. The Head Tender is currently your grandfather."

"I won't take anything," she said. "I'm not a thief."

"Swear it," Sage demanded. "Swear it on your life."

She was fully awake now. "I swear it. I swear it on my life!" She spoke so loudly that it sent her into a coughing fit.

"Poor little thing. We'll get you better in no time." Walnut smiled reassuringly. "Now, go and place your hand on that mountain."

Isabelle climbed down from the driver's bench.

The rock wall looked as smooth and black as an umbrella. She glanced back at her great-uncle, who nodded encouragingly. She reached out and placed her palm against the cold surface. A delicate vibration arose, growing stronger and stronger. The wall began to move. Isabelle darted behind an ox's head, watching over its twitching ears as black leaves popped out from the wall. The leaves continued to emerge until they had formed a large patch. Then they fanned out, revealing a tunnel.

"Well done," Walnut said, clapping his hands. Even Sage was smiling. "Only a tender's warm hands can do that. Those plants are called Camouflage Creepers."

Sage leapt from the caravan. "Follow me," he told Isabelle. With Rolo on his shoulder, he led the oxen through the tunnel. Once everyone had passed through, the leaves shuddered and the tunnel entrance closed. The travelers stood in total darkness.

"I've got one here somewhere. Just a moment," Walnut mumbled, searching his pockets. "Right. Found it." He pulled out a glowing blade of grass. The light bounced off the tunnel walls.

Isabelle followed Sage as they made their way. Eve the cat meowed from inside the caravan, so Walnut opened a little window behind the driver's seat and she leapt onto his lap.

The tunnel ended at a ridge. Isabelle ran in front of Sage. Emptiness lay before her as time hung between the moon's departure and the sun's arrival. *Nothing*, she thought. Just a big fat disappointment after all.

Nothing. No one. Nowhere.

But with the first trickle of dawn, Isabelle's heart soared. All the thousands of times she had imagined Nowhere, it had never looked like this.

Walnut stood on the driver's bench and held out his hands. "Welcome, Isabelle Fortune. Welcome to Fortune's Farm."

Chapter Eighteen
THE COLORS OF ISABELLE

A rosy glow crowned the distant mountain, then spread across the sky like spilled dye. Isabelle clutched Rocky to her chest as tendrils of gold and red washed down the mountain as fast as a coursing river, illuminating the valley below. An "ooh" and an "ahh" slid from her lips, for no words could express her amazement.

The birds awoke. A delicate twitter was joined by another, quickly building to a symphony of song. Rolo added his own notes as he flew off.

Though she didn't want to, Isabelle had to turn away and shut her eyes. The light had become too much to bear. The marmot wiggled from her grasp and jumped to the ground.

"You need these." Walnut pressed something against her nose. "Sunglasses, my dear." He slid the ends over her ears. "You can open your eyes now. But don't look directly at the sun. Never do that."

The sun.

Isabelle opened her eyes. The glasses felt strange but the brightness didn't hurt anymore. She looked out over the ridge.

The valley came to life in soft yellow light. A meadow sparkled with morning dew. A stream meandered through, criss-crossed by brightly painted bridges. To the right lay an orchard with trees planted in perfect rows. Their tops jiggled as songbirds continued their morning exultation. To the left lay a checkerboard garden, with little dirt paths between the plantings. Past the meadow sat an enormous glass building, a red barn, and a thatched roof cottage where smoke trailed from a chimney. A stone tower stood behind the cottage. Its little thatched roof looked like a hat. At the edge of the valley, just below the mountain, sat a lake shaped like a half round of cheese with an island in the middle.

Still, Isabelle couldn't find the words. "It's so . . . It's so . . ."

"Beautiful?" Walnut asked.

"More than that." .

"Splendiferous?"

"Much, much more."

"Hmmm." Walnut removed his knit hat and scratched his bald spot. "Radiant? Dazzling? Breathtakingly stupendous?"

"No. It's . . . *delicious.*"

And so it was, for Isabelle's puckered skin drank up the sun's rays like a dried-out sea sponge drinks salt water. She rolled up the kelp suit's sleeves and held out her arms. So this was what it felt like to be warm all over — like an enormous hug. She wanted to feel the sun on her face, so she took off the sunglasses. Something had changed and she didn't seem to need them any longer.

Walnut pulled his glasses from his pocket and perched them on his nose. "How interesting," he whispered, gazing through the thick lenses. "My oh my. What an unexpected change. Your eyes, my dear. They've turned green."

"My eyes?"

Walnut stepped closer. "And your skin. Take a look."

Isabelle inspected her arm. The skin that had always been as puckered as a dried-up slug and as pale as moonlight, looked smooth and slightly pink. Her other arm had transformed in the same way and the mold patches had disappeared. "You look lovely. Sage, doesn't she look lovely?"

Sage stared from behind his tangled hair. Isabelle felt certain he'd tell her she was still as ugly as ever. But he just stared.

"Sage? Isn't she lovely?"

Sage looked down at his feet. "I don't know."

"Of course you know. Just look at her. Why, she's radiant."

Sage cringed. "She looks . . . better, I guess." He turned away. "What do I care what she looks like, anyway?" He and the oxen started down the path, with Eve the cat leading the way. Rocky the marmot followed, scurrying here and there, stopping to smell ox poop and everything else she encountered.

"Come," Walnut said, tipping his hat. "There's so much to show you."

The path continued its steep decline, then leveled at the edge of the orchard. Sage unhooked the oxen. As they lumbered off, he shot Isabelle another puzzled look. *He can barely stand to look at me,* she thought. *I'm the ugliest girl he's ever seen.*

"I'm starving. I need some breakfast," Sage said. Abandoning the caravan, he ran off through the trees. Eve the cat hissed at the marmot, then followed Sage, bounding down the orchard path with her tail perched regally in the air.

"Don't mind him," Walnut said, taking Isabelle's hand. "We haven't had a girl around this farm in a very long time. Just been us three boys. Sage doesn't quite know how to act around girls. I'm sure he doesn't mean to be so rude."

"No other girls?" He must have misspoken. "But what about my mother?"

Walnut let Isabelle's hand drop. "Ah, your mother." He looked away. "I'm sorry to tell you, dear Isabelle, but it's just your grandfather and me. We are all the family you have."

"What do you mean?" Isabelle leaned against the caravan, feeling faint. "I don't have a mother or father?"

"Not any longer. Are you terribly disappointed?"

No mother? No father? Of course she was disappointed! She wanted to cry but she held back the tears. She pressed her lips together to keep the disappointment inside. After all, a grandfather and a great-uncle were more relatives than she had ever had in her entire life. So, she put on a brave little smile. "I'm not . . . terribly disappointed. But what happened to them?"

Walnut sighed. "We can talk about that later. Right now we both need some breakfast. Fortunately, there's plenty to eat right here." He spread his arms. "You've come at the peak of fruit season."

Aside from the occasional apple at the factory store, the only fruit Isabelle had ever seen came in a tin labeled FRUIT COCKTAIL. Mama Lu served the treat to her tenants once a year, on her birthday. Before serving, she would inspect each bowl and pick out the cherries. "Them's fer me," she'd shout. "I'm the birthday girl." Then she'd pick out the green grapes and the pears. "You all can have the peaches. I hate them peaches."

Fruit in all shapes and sizes crowded the branches of the orchard trees. Some were golden, some orange, some striped red and white. Rocky sank her big front teeth into a purple fruit that had fallen to the ground. Isabelle's spirits lifted as she pointed down the lane. "Are those Love Apples?"

"Yes. Help yourself."

Isabelle's mouth watered as she hurried to the tree, remembering the last juicy bite she had taken, which seemed like a lifetime ago. Dozens of red apples hung between shiny green leaves but the twisted branches grew too high for Isabelle's reach, even on tiptoe. "How do I get one?"

"You're a tender," Walnut said, pulling a root out of his nose. "All you have to do is ask."

Ask? But hadn't he already given her permission to take one? "Great-Uncle Walnut, may I . . ."

"No, no." He chuckled. "Ask the tree." He wandered back to the caravan, leaving Isabelle to ponder this latest mystery.

Considering how much she wanted an apple, asking rather than taking did seem like the polite thing to do. Isabelle stepped closer to the knotted trunk. She didn't know exactly what to look for — a face maybe, or a pair of ears sticking out of the wood. "Um, hello, tree." She felt a bit silly. While she had had long conversations with barnacles, potato bugs, and slugs, she had never before spoken to a tree. This was not a prejudice on Isabelle's part — trees simply did not grow in Runny Cove. "I was wondering if I could have one of your apples for breakfast?"

You may. The voice, wispy like a cloud, floated through the leaves. A little shiver ran up Isabelle's neck.

The tree gracefully lowered a branch until it hung at Isabelle's shoulder. She smiled and gently plucked an apple. "Thank you."

You're welcome, Tender. The branch retreated.

Isabelle took a hungry bite. Just as tasty as the one that had traveled in Neptune's nose.

Walnut stepped out of the caravan and held up a little bag. It swayed in his hand. "Look what I found," he called, hurrying over to Isabelle. He untied the bag and humming burst forth, louder than before and much more urgent. "The little fellow is angry. Thinks we forgot him."

Isabelle had forgotten all about the seed. But who could blame her with all the distractions? The tree began to shake all over, rustling its leaves excitedly. Walnut pinched the seed between his fingers. The root, which had doubled in size, wiggled like an earthworm. "That's a mighty fine seed," Walnut said, pushing the glasses up his nose. "Mighty fine. Best get it planted."

He took a small trowel from his coat pocket and dug a hole. The tree leaned over to get a better view. "You should do the honors," Walnut told Isabelle. "It's your seed, after all."

Isabelle squatted next to him. "What do I do?"

"Let your instincts guide you." He smiled confidently. "You may be uneducated in our ways but instinct is a powerful source of knowledge."

She carefully laid the humming seed in the hole. The moment its root touched dirt, the seed released an enormous sigh, as did the tree. Isabelle filled the hole and patted the dirt into place.

"No need to water," Walnut said. "Our rain cloud passes over at noon each day."

For much of the morning, Isabelle followed her great-uncle around the orchard, eating everything the trees offered. Walnut rattled off names — Klondike Kumquat, Forever Fig, Angelic Apricot, and Passion Plum — but Isabelle was too caught up in the feast to keep track. She ate and ate until she thought her kelp pants might split. Rocky ate until all she could do was clutch her bloated yellow belly and groan.

"This is a Magnetic Mango," Walnut said, handing Isabelle a yellow fruit. "Comes in handy on lengthy journeys because it takes so long to digest. Eat one before setting out. The mango will buzz when your stomach points north so you'll never get lost." He stopped beneath a tree covered in little red fruits. "Oh, you must eat these. Tree, may we have some of your cherries?" The tree obliged and Walnut handed one of its fruits to Isabelle. "This is the Curative Cherry. It cures the common cold and serious secondary infections such as *Pneumonia Stubbornia*. Go on. You'll feel better immediately. It will clear that stuffy nose and get rid of that cough."

Isabelle had no idea what a clear nose felt like, or what it meant to be rid of a cough. The only way to get rid of a cough in Runny Cove was to die. She was so eager to find out if it worked that she almost broke a tooth on the hard round seed.

"Nibble around the pit," Walnut advised. He demonstrated, spitting the pit onto the ground. It instantly took root. "I have to be very careful with fruit. Most tenders can eat seeds but not me. Did you ever hear the story about the boy who ate a watermelon seed and a watermelon grew in his stomach?" Isabelle shook her head, finishing the rest of her cherry. "People will tell you not to believe such stories but I'm afraid it's true. You see, I was that boy." He lifted his coat and shirt. A silvery scar lay across his belly. "Don't want to go through that again."

Isabelle's nose tingled. She sniffed. "What's that?" She sniffed again. "I smell something. What is it?"

Walnut spat out another pit. "I imagine you're smelling *everything*."

Until that moment, only strong odors had been able to fight their way up Isabelle's nose — like the saltiness of the cove, the sourness of Mama Lu's cabbage soup, or the spiciness of Sage's cinnamon tea. But there, in the orchard, softer scents drifted in — warm, sweet, drowsy scents.

But that was not all. Isabelle's lungs, which had always felt heavy and wet, also cleared. She took a long, deep breath. The scratchy sensation that had always been in her throat faded away. She smiled. How great the villagers of Runny

Cove would feel if they each ate a Curative Cherry. Gwen wouldn't have that runny nose anymore. Mr. Limewig wouldn't wake up everyone with his coughing. "Can I give these to my friends?"

"I'm afraid that's problematic. You see, we have the only Curative Cherry tree in the world. It's one of our most guarded secrets. If certain people found out about the Curative Cherry they'd set out to destroy it. There's far too much money to be made with the common cold. Why, think of all the tissue factories, and nose spray factories, and throat drop factories that would be put out of business."

"But couldn't I take just a few? I wouldn't tell my friends about the farm."

"You'd have to get the Head Tender's permission — your grandfather. But he's not much for giving permission these days and we hardly ever see him. We . . ." Walnut stopped talking. "I think I'm seeing things." He cleaned his glasses on his coat hem, then perched them back on his nose. "I'm not seeing things," he whispered, staring at her.

"What's the matter?"

Walnut excitedly led Isabelle through the orchard to a blue bridge, where a creek widened into a still pool. "Look into the mirror pond," he said, pointing at the pool.

Isabelle knelt at the bridge's edge. The water below reflected the blue sky above. She leaned as far as she could until a face stared back at her. She gasped. "There's a girl in the water."

"There's no girl in the water. Look again."

It took Isabelle a few moments to recognize her own re-flection. She had never seen herself with smooth skin, or green eyes, or pink cheeks. Nor had she ever seen herself with anything but gray hair. "My hair!" she cried.

"Yes, your hair." Walnut clapped gleefully. "No tender has had hair that color since the very first tender." He danced a little jig. The bridge shook as he kicked up his feet. "It's a sign. A verifiable, delightful, wonderful sign."

Isabelle stared at her hair, once thin and lifeless, now thick and green.

Walnut twirled, almost falling off the bridge in the process. Then he gave Isabelle a mighty hug. "If this doesn't cheer your grandfather up, I don't know what will."

Chapter Nineteen

A NEW HOME

Her belly bulging, her skin shining, and her hair glowing, Isabelle followed her great-uncle to the thatched roof cottage. Just as he reached for the knob, the door burst open and Sage hurried out. "Got to do my rounds," Sage said, throwing some rope over his shoulder. Then he did a double take. "Isabelle? Is that you?"

"Yep." As proud as she felt of her new colors, she held back her smile, wondering what Sage's reaction would be. Would he make fun of her? Green hair is a bit unusual, after all.

He shuffled in place for what seemed a very long time before saying, "You don't look half bad. See ya in a few days." He hurried off.

"Be careful," Walnut called.

"Where's he going?" Isabelle asked. A few days was the length of time she had known Sage, and she realized that she would miss him.

Walnut waved as Rolo the raven flew in Sage's direction. "Off to do security rounds, to make sure the perimeter is secure. One hole in the dome and Mr. Supreme's hooligans could find their way in."

"You have a dome?"

"Not just any dome. An invisible dome. It's a magical barrier that keeps outsiders from wandering onto the farm."

"I see," Isabelle said, but she didn't, really. Just another amazing fact she'd have to accept, and she expected that the day would provide many more.

Walnut showed Isabelle to a room, tucked away at the end of a crooked hall. It was about the same size as the room on the fourth floor of Mama Lu's Boarding House, except that streaming sunlight illuminated its far wall, making it seem much bigger. "This will be your room."

"My room?" Those words sounded so strange. "Just mine?"

"Certainly," Walnut replied, tapping his dirt-stained fingers together. "It belongs to you."

Isabelle thought that maybe she had ferns growing in her ears. "An entire room belongs to me?"

"Of course. And everything in it belongs to you, too." Everything included a small bed covered in a bright quilt made from cotton gardening gloves, a stand of dusty shelves that waited to be filled, a cluster of candles, and a box of matches on a bedside table. Except for the rain slicker and boots she had purchased with her factory wages, nothing had ever belonged to Isabelle. Her clothes were hand-me-downs, on loan until she outgrew them.

The marmot crawled under a pillow. "I guess you've got a roommate," Walnut said.

Suddenly, Isabelle panicked. Could this be too good to be true? "How much is the rent?" Her great-uncle probably didn't realize that she didn't have any money. The few pennies she had saved and had hidden beneath her mattress now belonged to Mama Lu.

"Forgive me, my dear." Walnut poked his finger in his ear. A few bits of dirt tumbled out. "Did you ask about the *rent*?"

"Yes. How much is it?"

He frowned. "You don't pay rent. You're family. However, you will be expected to do your fair share of chores. And there are lots of chores to do around here. Too many, in fact, ever since your grandfather fired all the farmhands. The whole place is falling apart."

"Well, I'm a real good worker," Isabelle said proudly. "I can work for eight hours without taking a break."

"Why would anyone work eight hours without taking a break? Breaks are mandatory around here, as are naps, daydreams, and occasional episodes of goofing off." He opened the closet. A few pairs of pants and some shirts hung on wooden pegs. "There are some old clothes of Sage's in here, worn before his last growth spurt. They belong to you now. I'm afraid we don't have any girl clothes. My brother got rid of all your mother's belongings after . . . Well, not to worry about that right now." Walnut looked away.

Isabelle didn't need to be a rocket scientist — or any kind of scientist — to deduce the following: that the subject of her mother was a delicate one, perhaps an unpleasant subject. Had something horrible happened to her? And to her father? Though Walnut tried to avoid the answers, Isabelle was determined to know. She needed to know. She'd ask again, when the moment seemed right.

"There's a bathroom in here, just for you." Walnut opened a blue door.

Isabelle nearly tripped over her own feet as she rushed into the brightly painted bathroom. "Just for me?" No waiting in line behind the Limewigs and Wormbottoms in the cold hallway, wondering if they'd left any paper. No stumbling down two flights of stairs in the dark.

Walnut pointed to a sink shaped like a flower. "There's a towel over there, and some soap."

Would the wonders never cease? Not a ball of smooshed-together bits and pieces from Mama Lu's old soaps, but an entire bar of brand new soap, just for her.

"Why don't you change out of that kelp suit and clean up. Then you can explore the farm." Walnut gave Isabelle a big hug. "You have no idea, my dear. No idea how much you are needed. I thought that all was lost but here you are. You've made an old man very happy." His eyes misted. "I'm so glad that Sage found you." He hugged her again, then closed the bedroom door on his way out.

"I'm glad he found me, too," Isabelle whispered. Then she spun around, twirling like a seed in the wind. Her very own bedroom, her very own bathroom — rent-free!

Isabelle's little bathroom contained a shower that worked by pumping a handle. She peeled off the kelp suit and sighed as warm water cascaded over her new skin. The shower's basin turned gray as the final remnants of Runny Cove washed away. *My old self*, she thought, as gray swirled down the drain.

She dried herself with the fluffy towel. Not a dishrag like the ones at Mama Lu's, but a towel that reached from her nose to her toes. She dressed in a pair of tan cotton pants that fit well, a white cotton shirt, and a pair of soft boots. She found a comb and ran it through her new, thick hair. Gwen wouldn't even recognize her.

Poor Gwen. She'd be working in the Handle Room, attaching handles to the new colorful umbrellas. And Leonard would be working in the Testing Room, dumping buckets of water onto each umbrella to make certain it worked. Didn't they each deserve a warm shower, a fluffy towel, and a brand-new bar of soap?

I don't want to feel sad, Isabelle thought. *I can't help them right now but I will help them. Right now I just want to feel happy.* So she pushed the sad thoughts from her mind and looked out her bedroom window.

A grassy yard dotted with daisies stretched between her room and the red barn. Someone had parked the caravan next to the barn. Chickens made their way across the yard, clucking and pecking, and a pair of milk goats rested in the sun.

Fortune's Farm is the happiest place on earth, Isabelle thought. Her head filled with music and, right then and there, she made up a song. The chickens picked up the song's rhythm as they scratched the dirt.

The Fortune's Farm Song

I never thought that life could feel
warm and dry and bright.
I never knew that things could smell
sweet and clean and light.
But now I know and it's clear to me
that Fortune's Farm is the place to be.

Sunshine shining down,
songbirds flying round,
seedlings in the ground,
magic to be found,
here on Fortune's Farm.

I always hoped one day I'd find
a place to call my own.
I always prayed for a sign
to tell me where to go.
But now I'm here and it's clear to me
that Fortune's Farm is the place to be.

"Come on, Rocky," Isabelle said, opening the door. "Let's go explore."

The marmot crawled out from under the pillow and followed Isabelle down the crooked hall. They passed a door with a large "W" painted on it. Then they came to a door with a large "N" painted on it. Isabelle didn't mean to eavesdrop, but the voices behind the second door thundered.

"I don't believe you," said a man.

"You must believe me." That voice sounded like Walnut's. "We have a future now. We have hope."

"Why do you persist with this futile fantasy? We have no future. There's nothing more to be said." Sadness hung in the unknown voice. "The end has come. Now leave me in peace."

"But Nesbitt . . ."

"Enough!" he hollered. "I just want to be left alone. Go away."

Isabelle thought she might be reprimanded for listening and the last thing she wanted, on her first day in her new home, was to get into trouble. She hurried down the hall but as she did the unknown voice said, "The end has come."

"But Nesbitt . . ."

"THE END HAS COME!"

Chapter Twenty
THE DARK WINDOW

To whom did that angry voice belong? Great-Uncle Walnut had called him Nesbitt. Surely he couldn't be Isabelle's grandfather, for she had imagined him to be kind, gentle, and good-natured. And finding a lost grand-daughter would make for happiness and rejoicing, not yell-ing about things coming to an end. What had he meant by that, anyway?

While wondering about these latest mysteries, Isabelle stood in the Fortunes' kitchen, which was everything a kitchen should be — warm, colorful, and filled with tempt-ing scents. A wood-fed stove sat in the corner. Pots and pans hung from the beamed ceiling. Sun streamed in through open windows. Nothing in the room reminded her of Mama Lu's kitchen, which was damp and sticky, riddled with piles of salt, and filled with constant demands about wanting to hear something *interesting*. Since leaving Runny Cove, Isabelle had encountered enough *interesting* to make Mama Lu's head explode!

The Fortunes' kitchen also happened to be a complete mess, which didn't bother Isabelle one bit. Plates sat stacked in the sink and a family of mice ran along a little trail they had made across the dirt-covered floor. Red-breasted and black-crested birds flew in through the windows, helping themselves to overturned bags of corn meal and hazelnuts. Bees flew in and out of a doorless icebox that sat unplugged and empty, except for a mud-packed hive that dripped with golden syrup.

While the marmot dug a hole in a potted plant, Isabelle peered into some drawers. The first was filled with fat green worms. The second contained polka-dotted melons. One squirted at her; the stinky fluid just missed her shirt. She went to open another drawer but its contents growled fiercely. Best not to look in there.

A door slammed. Walnut emerged from the hallway, his face scarlet, swinging his arms and breathing hard as if he had just climbed to the fourth floor.

"Hello," Isabelle said, ducking as a songbird flew by. "I'm all clean and ready to explore."

But Walnut didn't bother to look up. "Stubborn old fool," he mumbled, stomping right past Isabelle and out the front door.

"Great-Uncle Walnut?" she called. "Come on, Rocky. Let's see where he's going." Isabelle pulled the marmot from her new hole.

Outside the thatched roof cottage, Isabelle looked for her great-uncle. She called his name but only a goat answered, bleating as it ambled toward the field. Rocky wiggled free and started digging another hole.

Where had Walnut gone? She looked around one side of the cottage. The barn sat quiet, its double doors closed. "Great-Uncle Walnut?" She ran to the other side, a wilder side with a forest and looming mountains, hoping for a trace of checkered coat and white hair. Still no sign of him.

She sighed. She'd have to explore on her own, but she had plenty of experience doing just that. Maybe she'd find some interesting things to put on those dusty shelves.

A tall post stood near the forest's edge, covered in arrow-shaped signs. THIS WAY TO THE LAKE SHAPED LIKE A HALF ROUND OF CHEESE. THIS WAY TO THE SWAMP THAT MAKES RUDE NOISES. THIS WAY TO THE CAVE THAT SWALLOWS THINGS THEN SPITS THEM BACK OUT. She pushed aside some tall blades of grass to read the last sign. THIS WAY TO THE TENDER AND FARMHAND CEMETERY. The arrow pointed down an overgrown path, its stepping stones barely visible. She had only visited Runny Cove's cemetery one time, a sad and eerie place of cracked headstones and prickly thornbushes. Maybe she'd find some answers about the rest of her family in Tenders' Cemetery. It was worth a try.

"Rocky," she called, hoping the marmot would join her. A cemetery would surely be less creepy with a furry friend by her side. But Rocky didn't appear, so Isabelle took a deep breath and set off down the trail.

A solitary dark cloud hung gloomily over the cemetery. Many of the headstones stood as tall as Isabelle. She wandered around, peeling back ivy vines to read the engravings. Dozens of Fortunes had been buried there, some of whom Walnut had mentioned and others, like Caesar Ragweeder Fortune, Pollenminder Veritas Fortune, and Sunflowery Millicent Fortune. Etched beneath each name was the cause of death: DIED MOST UNEXPECTEDLY FROM A FALL OFF A LADDER. DIED MOST PEACEFULLY WHILE NAPPING AT A

PICNIC. DIED MOST REGRETTABLY IN A DRUNKEN DUEL. Only one tombstone did not list cause of death and its single name read: DAFFODILLY.

In a separate part of the cemetery she found a clump of headstones that bore only single names like Bob, Poke, Curly, and Gus, followed by the statement, A LOYAL FARM-HAND TO HIS DYING DAY. These also mentioned cause of death, though in one-word form only: EATEN, SQUEEZED, SPONTANEOUSLY COMBUSTED, LOST. No doubt about it — farmhanding was a dangerous occupation.

Isabelle searched and searched but no headstone read: MOTHER TO ISABELLE or FATHER TO ISABELLE, or PARENTS OF THE CHILD WHO WAS LEFT ON A DOORSTEP. Walnut hadn't said that her parents had died. He said she *no longer* had a mother and father. That could mean something else besides death, couldn't it? Maybe. Hopefully.

A whistle rang through the cemetery. Isabelle, who was becoming something of a *Marmoticus Terriblus* expert, knew that marmots chirp when discussing things and whistle when they feel threatened. She ran back up the trail to the thatched-roof cottage. Maybe that goat was getting too close to Rocky's new hole. Another whistle sounded from somewhere in the field. "Rocky?" She stood on tiptoe and strained her green eyes, searching for a furry brown head. At the center of the field, something orange rose out of the grass, hovered in the air, then sank back down. Rocky whistled again.

Isabelle hurried across a red bridge. Not too far ahead,

another orange object floated above the grass, hovered, then disappeared. Heading that way, she crossed a green bridge and came to a pond. "Rocky," she cried out, relieved to find the marmot sitting at the water's edge. "What's the matter? I was worried."

Rocky squinted at the water. Orange fish, about the size of Mama Lu's salt canister, swam to the side of the pond and stared up at Isabelle with bulging black eyes. They swam in place, huddling together, shiny scale against shiny scale. "Fish," Isabelle said. While she had heard many stories from her grandmother, she had never been face to face with a real fish. She lay on the bank, resting her chin on her arms, watching them as intently as they watched her. Rocky climbed onto Isabelle's head for a better view. Were these the same kind of fish that Grandma Maxine's father used to catch in Runny Cove?

One of the fish grew bored and swam to the center of the pond, where it nibbled on a round-leafed plant. The fish took a few bites, then floated up out of the water. It didn't look surprised as it hovered. It flapped its tail and slowly sank back to its watery home. Grandma Maxine had never told her that fish could fly!

Rocky climbed off Isabelle's head and wandered closer to the edge, where she snagged one of the round leaves. She sank her buckteeth into the leaf's flesh, tapping her feet as she happily chewed. Apparently the pond plant made a delicious meal because she reached in and pulled out another.

Isabelle sat up and laughed, watching as another fish took a bite, then enjoyed a midair float. *What lucky fish,* Isabelle thought, *to be able to float like that.*

Rocky stopped chewing and chirped. She cocked her head, then rose off the ground. *It's the plant,* Isabelle realized, *not the fish.* "Oh Rocky, you shouldn't have eaten that plant."

The marmot whistled and frantically pawed at the air. Apparently, while goldfish enjoy mid-air floating, marmots do not. Isabelle leapt to her feet and tried to grab Rocky's stubby tail, but she was already out of reach. Squealing and writhing, the furry rodent rose higher and higher.

"You'll be fine," Isabelle called. "You'll come down soon." *Hopefully.* "Don't be afraid." A silly sight, to look up in the sky and see a marmot rump floating past, but Isabelle felt too worried to giggle. Rocky was her friend, her responsibility. The slugs and the potato bugs had died because she hadn't been strong enough to fight Mama Lu. And she hadn't been brave enough to fight Mr. Supreme. Had she been, she could have gotten home in time to save her grandmother. She wasn't about to let anything happen to her marmot. She ran as quickly as she could, following the marmot's shadow. If Rocky fell . . .

But Rocky didn't fall. Isabelle held out her arms as the trembling rodent descended. "You scared me." After a wet nose kiss, Rocky wiggled free of Isabelle's hug and scampered off. "Don't eat anything else," Isabelle called.

Though that advice seemed wise for a marmot, Isabelle found herself wondering what it would feel like to float, not across an ocean, but on air. She wandered back to the pond. No sign read: DON'T EAT THE PLANTS. No one stood there yelling, "Yer not supposed to float, ya hear me? Keep yer nasty little hands off my plants!" Isabelle reached into the water and pulled out a leaf. It tasted bitter, but nothing happened. She ate another leaf, then another. *Maybe I'm too big*, she thought.

Her body went numb. She knew she still had legs because she could see them, but it felt as if they had run off. It felt as if her entire body had drifted away.

Then her feet left the ground. Like the marmot, Isabelle grabbed at air, looking for something to hold on to. *Oh, what have I done?* She floated higher and higher but in a matter of moments she got used to her weightlessness and relaxed. *So this is what it feels like to be a cloud*, she thought, smiling. *Gwen and Leonard would love this!*

A breeze slid beneath her, lifting and carrying her back toward the cottage. Her white shirt billowed as she drifted. She moved her arms and legs but couldn't quite figure out how to control direction — that probably took some practice. She rested her hands behind her head. Why would anyone bother to walk around the farm with floating as an option? If Great-Uncle Walnut allowed it, she'd eat those leaves every day.

The breeze carried her over the thatched-roof cottage. She drifted toward the tower that loomed behind the cottage, right up to its single dark window. Grabbing the window's ledge, she held herself in place and peered through the glass. A man sat hunched in front of a fire, his back to the window. Orange streaks ran through his short white hair. Eve the cat nestled beside him.

Isabelle knew, from the way he sat all curled up and small, that the man felt terribly sad. Most of the workers at the Magnificently Supreme Umbrella Factory sat in the same way.

"Isabelle, what are you doing up there?" Walnut stood in the yard, clutching a basket. "My oh my, you shouldn't be looking in that window. Come down, my dear."

"I don't know how to get down," Isabelle called back.

"Push away from that window before he sees you."

But it was too late. The man turned abruptly and all Isabelle noticed were his eyes, at first gentle and sleepy, but then they widened and blazed. His voice boomed through the glass panes. "How dare you. Get out of here!" He swept an arm toward her. "GO!"

Terrified, Isabelle let go of the ledge, but she didn't drift away. The air beneath the tower's overhanging roof was still and lifeless. She hovered as the angry man stormed his way to the window, his fists clenched.

Walnut cupped a hand over his mouth. "Can you hear me? You need to come down."

"I'm trying," Isabelle cried, kicking her legs. She wanted to get down more than anything. As the man glared out the window, she kicked with all her might, dislodging a clump of thatching in the process. Another kick and she managed to float free.

"Stay away from that window from now on," Walnut called. "And when the Floating Fronds wear off, meet me in the greenhouse." He pointed toward the immense glass building. "I've got to get these roots into some water right away." He hurried off.

"No, don't leave," Isabelle cried, but Walnut didn't seem to hear.

As she floated away from the tower, the angry man opened the window. "You're not wanted," he snarled. "Go away."

After a long, venomous look, he slammed the window closed and drew its curtain.

Chapter Twenty-One
THE SEED DEPOSITORY

You're not wanted.

As the Floating Fronds wore off, those hurtful words rang in Isabelle's head. "You're not wanted" is a rotten thing to say to a person who has just arrived. It had to be a misunderstanding. After all, Sage had traveled across the ocean to find her and Great-Uncle Walnut had been waiting with the caravan to greet her. They wouldn't have gone to so much trouble if she hadn't been wanted. That man in the tower must have mistaken her for someone else.

But who was he? And why was he so angry?

Isabelle glanced up at the tower window, now shaded by a curtain. If she walked to the uppermost room in the tower and introduced herself, said something like, "Hi, I'm Isabelle. I'm a tender and I'm very happy to meet you," then surely he'd smile and tell her that he had forgotten to put on his glasses and had mistaken her floating shape for a giant hornet or a storm cloud or something.

"Isabelle," Walnut called from the greenhouse. He waved a shiny blade in the air. "Come along. I've got so much work to do."

As Isabelle's feet touched the ground, the numbness wore off. Reunited with her body, she hurried across the yard to the large glass building. "Can I float like that every day?" she asked her great-uncle, who was plucking a daisy from his bald spot.

"Best not to overdo the floating. Too much and your body gets befuddled. I learned that when I was your age. Woke up one morning after a particularly long float and found that my hands thought that they were feet. And my toes thought that they were fingers. Have you ever tried squeezing lemonade with your toes?"

Isabelle shook her head.

"Makes your toes stick together. Don't recommend it." He raised the blade in the air. "Good thing I found my old machete. Now that we are without farmhands, the weeds have taken over. We'll have to hack our way through."

Hack, whack, hack. Walnut swung the blade from side to side, slicing through the fortress of tangled vines and leaves. Isabelle kept a good distance as her great-uncle's arm flew wildly about. Chopped bits of leaves sprayed onto her hair and face.

"Never . . . seen . . . it . . . this . . . bad." Walnut attacked a shrub that was putting up a fight. "Yet another reason why I will never find myself a wife. Difficult enough to find one when the farm was running smoothly, but now that the farm's falling apart I'm doomed to bachelorhood. What sort of woman would be willing to deal with this mess, day after day?" He grunted, swinging the blade above his head, then held it in midair. "You wouldn't happen to know any unmarried women in Runny Cove who have farm experience, would you?"

The only unmarried woman she knew, other than Mama Lu, was Gertrude, and even if she had "farm experience," and maybe she did, Isabelle wouldn't tell her great-uncle about it. No way was Gertrude coming to live on the farm.

"They're all married," she lied. It is perfectly acceptable to lie when it means saving someone from a fate worse than being eaten, squeezed, or spontaneously combusted.

"I suspected as much." With another grunt he brought the blade down upon a thorn-covered branch.

"My grandmother wasn't married. She's the one who found me." Isabelle ducked as a thorn flew past. "She died and the undertaker took her. You would have liked her."

"I'm sure I would have."

Beads of sweat trickled down Isabelle's neck. Though a gentle mist drifted from the ceiling it did not provide relief from the greenhouse's humidity. She wiped her forehead with her sleeve.

Walnut stopped hacking and wiped his forehead too. "The tropicals love this heat," he explained, catching his breath. "Especially this one." He plucked a yellow pod from a tree. "This is called a Suncatcher. I always try to keep one of these in my pocket. They come in handy when it gets cold." He cracked open the pod and sunlight spilled across his hand. "Great for warming up your bed. Once the sunlight is released, the pod evaporates." Which it did, right before Isabelle's eyes.

"Oh, and these are blades of Glow Grass." He picked a blade and stuffed it into his pocket. "I always keep a few in case I find myself in the dark." Isabelle remembered the blade from their trip through the tunnel.

"Great-Uncle Walnut," she said, shaking an incandescent beetle off her hand. "Who is that man in the tower?"

"Ah." Walnut paused thoughtfully. "His name is Nesbitt. Nesbitt Rhododendrol Fortune. My older brother. Your grandfather."

"My grandfather?" How could that be? "But he said that I wasn't wanted. He yelled at me to go away."

Walnut pulled loose a vine that had begun to curl around his neck. "Your grandfather has been in a bad mood lately. Well, for about ten years, to be exact. But he'll come around." He frowned. "That's our hope, anyway."

"Why would he want me to go away? Why isn't he happy to see me?"

"We can better discuss that in the Depository." He slid the machete into his belt. "I think we're nearing the end. Just have to get through this forest of Belchiferus Bamboo. I highly recommend that you hold your breath."

Walnut got to his knees and began to crawl between thick brown stalks. Isabelle followed, her hands pressing into the rich greenhouse soil. Burping sounds erupted overhead. Thin streams of black gunk oozed down the stalks. She couldn't hold her breath any longer.

"Yuck," she said as a noxious stench shot up her nose.

"That, my dear, is the bamboo's natural defense mechanism. Surprisingly, that secretion makes delightful pancake syrup. Ah, here we are."

He pushed aside some soil to reveal a small door, set in the floor. After pulling it open, he handed Isabelle a blade of

Glow Grass. They started down a steep flight of stairs, the air cooling with each step. "We've found it best to store our seeds underground. They can sleep down here for hundreds of years, if need be."

The stairs ended in a large room. While the Glow Grass was too dim to illuminate the room itself, it bounced off multiple pairs of red eyes. "This is the Seed Depository," Walnut announced as he lit a cluster of candles, bringing the room into view. The eyes belonged to a group of black squirrels, caught in the act of stuffing their cheeks with seeds. "Shoo!" Walnut said. The squirrels squeaked, then darted into various holes in the walls. "Thieving pests."

Like the kitchen, the depository was a mess. Boxes lay everywhere, some overturned, others stacked. The box closest to Isabelle read: LUNAR MOSS. COLLECTED WINTER, 1453. USED FOR LOVE ELIXIRS AND TERMITE MANAGEMENT. The box lay open and empty.

"Everything's out of order," Walnut said, throwing his hands in the air. "My seeds used to be alphabetized, but those squirrels keep moving everything around." He took two cotton gloves from his pocket and slid them onto his hands. Then he started picking seeds off the table. Isabelle realized that with his warm hands and his special ability to make everything grow quickly, he had to wear the gloves to keep the seeds from sprouting.

"Great-Uncle Walnut? My grandfather? Remember?"

Walnut sighed and dropped the seeds. "What's the use?" he asked. He pushed aside a box and sat on a stool. "New seeds are going to waste in the garden because I can't collect them fast enough. And old seeds are fattening up the local rodents." He hung his head over the table. "How can I do everything without any help? It's too much for an old man, I tell you. Too much."

Isabelle knew, all too well, what it felt like to be over-whelmed with work. She cleared away some boxes and sat on a stool next to her great-uncle. "I know lots of people who would love to come here and help you. Gwen and Leonard would make great farmhands. And so would Boris and Bert, but . . ." She stopped, remembering the tombstones and the horrible ways that some of the farmhands had died. "I don't want any of them to get eaten or squished."

"That hasn't happened since the turn of the century," he assured her. "But that's beside the point. No one can work here without the Head Tender's permission. And your grandfather is the current Head Tender. He's the one who decided that we didn't need farmhands any longer. He's the one who fired them."

"Why did he fire them?" she asked.

Walnut stared wearily at the far wall. "We can talk about that later."

"Later?" Isabelle couldn't take it any longer. All her life, her questions had gone unanswered. She wanted to know! She gripped the edge of the stool angrily. "Why did you bring me here if he doesn't want me? Why did Sage say that I might be the last tender?" Her voice rose with frustration. "Why won't anyone tell me anything about my parents?"

Walnut slowly removed his gloves and rested his hands on his knees, looking at Isabelle with a mixture of melancholy and confusion. "I'm not sure where to begin. There is so much to be told."

Just begin somewhere, Isabelle wanted to shout. "How about telling me why Sage brought me here?"

"Very well." He lifted a bucket from the floor and set it onto the table. Reaching in, he scooped out a handful of dirt. "Do you know what this is?"

"It looks like dirt."

"Exactly so. A tender couldn't do his or her job without dirt. It's one of the most important things on this planet."

Isabelle had never considered dirt important before. It was just something that she tracked in on her boots, or something that turned to mud in the rain. And Mama Lu was always yelling, "Get that dirt out of here, ya dimwit!"

"Sage brought me here because of . . . dirt?"

"I'm getting to it." He held out the handful of dirt. "Each evening before going to bed, a tender should always give thanks to the dirt."

Isabelle furrowed her brow. "Mama Lu said we should give thanks when she gets her cheese delivery. She says, 'Thank God for the cheese.'"

Even though it wasn't a joke, Walnut's face lit up and he chuckled. But Isabelle didn't feel like laughing. He still hadn't answered her question. Dropping the dirt back into the bucket, he continued. "I tell you this because while the rest of the world may have grown to hate dirt, you must always, always revere it. For once Nesbitt and I have passed on, you, Isabelle Fortune, will be the last tender. And if there is any hope for magic to return, it lies with you and you alone."

"With me?" She anxiously slid off the stool. "I don't know anything about magic. Are you sure there aren't any more tenders? Have you looked everywhere?"

"We don't need to look. The Fortunes have always been the only tenders. There is no reason to believe that any other tenders exist outside the family." He motioned for her to sit again and she did. "You see, there once was a time when magic was as accepted as, well, as cheese is accepted. While this Mama Lu person gets her cheese delivered by a delivery truck, the people of long ago had their magic delivered by a sorcerer. Sorcerers were powerful manipulators of magic, and as it happens with most things, some of them went bad."

"Cheese stinks when it goes bad."

"So does magic, figuratively speaking. The people turned against it and the sorcerers died off. Well, some were murdered. Some just drifted away." He leaned forward. "The very last sorcerer, a good sorcerer, upon realizing her fate, cast a spell over her farm to protect it from the hostile world. Her farm is this very farm we live on today. Thanks to her spell, our farm looks like solid mountain and feels like solid rock to outsiders. In fact, whenever a group of climbers come this way, they walk right overhead."

"That's amazing," Isabelle said, imagining looking out the window and seeing a group of people trekking across the sky.

"Before she departed, the last sorcerer entrusted the care and keeping of her magical plants and creatures to her gardener, a man named Wilhelm Fortune. He was the first tender, my dear. Your distant relation."

"The one with the green hair?"

"The very one."

"And she never came back? The sorcerer?"

"Never." Walnut leaned even closer, his green eyes twinkling with candlelight. "But we have always believed that one day she will return, and magic will take its rightful place in the world again. So we tenders continue to do what we do best, while keeping the farm a secret from the world."

The table lightly shook and some dirt fell from the ceiling. "What's happening?" Isabelle asked.

"It's another Supreme Gyrocopter," Walnut said. "Flying overhead. Don't worry. The dome will protect us."

"How does Mr. Supreme know about the farm?"

"Ah." Walnut's face fell into sadness. "That is the reason your grandfather is so angry. It's time I told you about your mother."

But just as Isabelle's heart revved up with expectation, Rolo flew in and dropped something on Walnut's head.

Chapter Twenty-Two
THE BROKEN PROMISE

After bouncing off Walnut's head, a wooden spool landed on the table. The raven landed beside it. Walnut examined the spool. "Oh, I see that Sage is out of thread. I'm not sure how much I have left." He hurried across the depository and opened a basket, searching through its contents.

Mrs. Wormbottom owned a spool of thread. She shared it with the other tenants when they needed to mend holes in their shirts or pants. Why would Sage need thread? "I thought Sage was doing a security check," Isabelle said.

"He is. Aha, I found one." Walnut offered a new spool to Rolo but the bird turned away. "What? Not big enough? It's a big hole, is it?"

Rolo nodded.

Walnut sighed. "Oh dear, that's terrible news."

So what if Sage had a big hole in his pants? No way was that as important, or as interesting, as finding out about her mother. Isabelle fidgeted impatiently, wishing that the bird would just take the spool and fly away. But Rolo waited while Walnut rummaged through another basket.

"Terrible, terrible," Walnut mumbled. "Bigger and bigger holes. We never get a moment's peace around here." He presented an enormous spool, bigger than a marmot. Rolo hopped excitedly in place. "Isabelle, this spool is too heavy for Rolo to carry. Will you take it to Sage? I've got to get these seeds into storage. They're Snowfall Sweet Peas and if they're exposed to air for too long, we'll have snow in the middle of summer. Holes *and* snow. Don't want that."

"But you were going to tell me . . ."

"Yes, yes, about your mother. That can wait. Sage needs the thread. Hurry."

Isabelle grabbed the spool of black thread. It seemed absolutely ridiculous to rush off just because Sage had a stupid hole. In fact, it seemed . . . stupid!

"You must hurry," Walnut said, gently pushing her toward the stairs. "A hole is not to be messed around with."

"But I don't know where Sage is."

"Follow Rolo. Don't stray or dawdle, no matter how many interesting things you see along the way. Here." He pulled a sandwich from his pocket. "I made it this morning. Cucumber-butter."

Isabelle took the sandwich. "Will you tell me about my parents when I get back?"

"Yes. Now go."

"Do you promise?"

"Yes, yes." He flapped his hands in the air, urging her up the stairs.

Great-Uncle Walnut did not seem like the sort of person who would break a promise. Even so, Isabelle scowled. She had come so close to learning about her mother and now she had to run a ridiculous errand. She shoved the spool under her arm and followed Rolo up the stairs, under the Belchiferus Bamboo, and down the hacked greenhouse path.

A little cloud hovered outside the greenhouse door, dropping rain onto a barrel in which red flowers grew. Then the cloud moved to a barrel of yellow flowers. It was the cloud that Walnut had mentioned, the one that watered the farm, for no other clouds hung in the mid-day sky. Isabelle stood outside the greenhouse, her bad mood instantly washed away by the sun's warmth. Would it always take her by surprise? Even after years of living on the farm would she still marvel at it? She began to hum, *Sunshine shining down, songbirds flying 'round, seedlings in the ground, magic to be found, here on Fortune's Farm.*

She wanted to share the sun with Gwen and Leonard. Would all the gray wash off their bodies? What would they look like with smooth skin? Would they love her new home as much as she did? Of course they would. Who wouldn't love dry clothes, floating fronds . . .

. . . and a grumpy old man who was opening the tower window?

"I told you to go away!" He leaned out and shook his fist.

"Bu . . . bu . . . but I'm your granddaughter," she stammered.

"I don't care who you are. The end has come, so go away!" He popped his orange-streaked head back inside and slammed the window shut.

Raindrops rolled down Isabelle's face. The little cloud hovered over her head. She walked to the right, it floated to the right. She ran to the left, it quickly floated to the left. Just great. It had mistaken her for a green shrub. As the cloud watered Isabelle, her heart sank. If her grandfather didn't want her to stay, he certainly wouldn't welcome her friends. All her life she had wanted to find Nowhere and there she stood, smack dab in the middle of it. But she couldn't call it home — not yet. There had to be a way to change his mind. If only she knew why he was so angry.

Being "special" didn't mean squat when it came to getting questions answered.

Rolo circled, cawing for Isabelle to follow. The sooner she delivered the spool to Sage, the sooner she could get back and continue the conversation with her great-uncle. "Rocky," she called. Where was that marmot?

Rocky hung over the side of a trough, drinking water. A bearded goat nibbled on the marmot's stubby tail. "Come on, Rocky," Isabelle called.

Finally, the cloud moved on to a patch of brown grass.

Rolo led Isabelle and Rocky past the signpost to a trail that headed into the mountains. While Isabelle was used to climbing to the fourth floor, by the middle of the hike she felt as if she had climbed to the forty-fourth floor. Even Rocky grew tired and lay on her belly, panting wheezily. They took a break, sharing the cucumber-butter sandwich as Rolo pruned his feathers in a treetop.

Her strength renewed, Isabelle perched the marmot on her shoulder and set off again. Each step took her further away from her great-uncle and his promised answers. With each step she grew more and more annoyed that Sage hadn't come to get the spool of thread himself. So when she finally found him, sitting on the ground with his satchel at his side, she was all scowls and irritation. "Here." She shoved the spool in his face.

"Thanks," he said. His gaze traveled over her face and hair. She readied herself for him to say something mean like, *What took you so long?* or *I never gave you permission to wear my old clothes,* or *You look even worse than you did before.* But he surprised her.

"I like your colors."

Isabelle stopped scowling. "You do?"

"Yeah. Green hair is kind of nice. Well, it sure beats gray. And your eyes don't look so sad. You're not so . . . so . . ." He rolled the spool between his hand. "I mean, you look kinda . . . kinda . . ." His voice changed, like he was fighting with each word. "Well, you know, you're . . . you're . . ." He cleared his throat. "Not ugly."

What a nice thing to say. Isabelle's face went hot and she felt bad about shoving the spool at him. "Thanks." She ran her fingers through her thick hair. "They won't even recognize me when I go back to Runny Cove."

He began to unwind the thread. "Why would you go back to Runny Cove? It's the most horrible place I've ever seen."

Isabelle scratched the marmot's head. "Well, I think that there are plenty of Curative Cherries in the orchard. I could give one to everybody and they wouldn't be sick anymore. And then I'll bring my friends back with me. There's plenty of room and Great-Uncle Walnut said that he can't get all the work done without some help."

"You can't do any of those things without the Head Tender's permission. You made the solemn promise not to tell anyone about the farm and not to take anything from the farm. You have to speak to the Head Tender. Have you spoken to him yet?"

"No, not really." She shuffled her feet, embarrassed by what she was about to admit. "He yelled at me. He told me to go away. Why doesn't my grandfather like me? Did I do something wrong?"

"Not you. Someone else." He stopped unwinding and tucked a rope of hair behind his ear. "Your grandfather has given up, Isabelle. He fired the farmhands because he thinks there's no future for magic or the farm. He's waiting to die and for the farm to die. That's why all the plants are overgrown and why the garden is filled with weeds. That's why the seeds are rotting and why the squirrels are getting fat. But Walnut and I don't want the farm to die. Walnut believes that magic will have a place in the world again, and I . . . well, this is the only home I've ever had. So we went to find you, hoping that if Nesbitt met you, he'd believe in our future again."

"But he doesn't want to meet me. He told me to go away."

"We're hoping that you'll be able to change his mind." He threaded a silver needle. Then he stuck the needle into the air, pulled it, and stuck it into the air again.

"What are you doing?"

"There's a hole in the dome," he said.

She leaned forward and looked at the place where he held

the needle. "I don't see a hole. It's just air. How can air have a hole?"

"You can't see the hole because you aren't trained to see it. But I've been doing this for five years now, so trust me. It's right there and it's big. If I don't fix it, it will get bigger and then someone could slip through and find the farm." He chewed on his lower lip, concentrating on his task.

"Can I help?"

"I only have one needle. But thanks."

Isabelle sat nearby, wishing she had another sandwich. "How come there's a hole?" she asked. "And don't tell me that I should know."

Sage's tangled hair hung down the back of his yellow shirt. His long legs didn't look so skinny in regular pants. "It goes back to that promise."

"Not to tell anyone about the farm and not to take anything from it."

"Yep. Every tender has to make that solemn promise. The sorcerer set it up that way. If a tender breaks the promise then the spell that protects the farm is weakened and you get holes. Walnut didn't have the Head Tender's permission when he told you about the farm, but that didn't weaken the spell because the sorcerer's magic recognizes you as a rightful heir to the knowledge. You're supposed to know the secret. You're supposed to be here. Besides, the holes started appearing a long time ago."

"Oh." Isabelle thought she saw a stitched seam hover in

the air in front of Sage's face, but then it disappeared. "Then who broke the promise?" Silence followed her question. She threw her hands up. "Oh great. I suppose you can't tell me. Of course not. No one tells me anything." She folded her arms. "If I'm supposed to be the last tender and the only hope for magic, or whatever, then shouldn't I know what's going on?"

"Yes, you should." He tied a knot and broke the thread with his teeth.

"Then tell me who broke the vow."

"I can't. Walnut wants to be the one to tell you."

Isabelle stood. "Then I'm going back. He said he'd answer my questions when I got back."

"Dusk will come before you're halfway down the mountain," Sage said, tucking the thread and needle into his satchel. "You could get lost. I'll go with you. Hey, wait for me."

Though her legs were tired and the marmot's claws dug into her shoulders, Isabelle ran down that mountain. She was going to learn the truth about her parents, once and for all, and the reason why she was the only person in Runny Cove to ever have been left on a doorstep.

Chapter Twenty-Three

DAFFODILLY FORTUNE

As the farm's songbirds tucked themselves into their nests, and the pantry mice curled by the fire, Isabelle, Great-Uncle Walnut, and Sage sat at the kitchen table. Walnut dipped a ladle into a cast iron pot, filling three bowls with steaming potato stew. Sage sliced through a yellow round of cheese, handing Isabelle a wedge-shaped chunk. Mama Lu had never shared her cheese. It crumbled in Isabelle's mouth, then melted into creamy deliciousness.

"You promised to tell me about my parents," Isabelle said.

"We will eat first," Walnut told her, blowing on his stew. "A tale of sadness is better endured on a full stomach."

So they ate — Isabelle as quickly as she could. Rocky, who had uprooted the potted plant and had tossed it aside, dug joyfully. No one seemed to care, so Isabelle didn't scold her.

Hurry up and eat. Hurry up and eat.

FINALLY, just when Isabelle thought she couldn't sit a moment longer, the time came. Walnut unbuttoned his plaid jacket and swept his long white hair behind his shoulders. He leaned back in his chair and folded his hands over his belly. He began like any good storyteller, with a first line certain to capture a listener's attention.

"Earthworms were especially fond of your mother."

Isabelle leaned forward. "Did you say earthworms?"

"I did, indeed. Even when she was a baby, whenever she

sat on the ground, all the earthworms would migrate toward her. Such a fantastic gift for a tender. She was a superb composter. Compost is derived from the Latin *compositus* or *compostus,* meaning to convert plant debris into dirt. Composting is a skill that all tenders must learn in order to condition the land for planting and to . . ."

Isabelle fidgeted. Sage cleared his throat.

"Oh." Walnut paused. "I guess you don't want to hear about that. You want to hear about your parents."

"Yes. Please."

Tears pooled on Walnut's lower lids. He wiped them away with his dirt-stained hands. Something had sprouted beneath one of his fingernails. "This subject always upsets me. I miss my niece so very much."

Sage busied himself in the kitchen, keeping his back turned as if to give Walnut and Isabelle a bit of privacy.

Walnut took a dingy handkerchief from his pocket and blew his nose. "You'd better sit down, my dear. The story is difficult to bear."

"I am sitting down."

"Then you'd better sit still. All that wiggling is very distracting. A story this terrible requires a great deal of concentration."

Isabelle sat stiff, her jaw clenched, preparing herself for what was sure to be the saddest story she had every heard — even sadder than Grandma Maxine's story about how Sunny Cove had become Runny Cove.

"Your mother's name was Daffodilly because she was

born in March, the time when daffodils bloom here in the north. She was a beautiful, healthy baby, and did all the usual baby things, like sleeping in trees, tunneling underground, and floating."

Isabelle wasn't certain, but those didn't sound like *usual* baby things.

"When Daffodilly turned ten, the time came to send her away for schooling. Mrs. Fortune chose to send her to Madame Pungent's School for Girls in Switzerland, her own alma mater. It's always difficult for tender parents to send their children into the outside world, but a good education is of the utmost importance. Daffodilly received excellent grades and came home for winter and summer breaks. All went well until her seventeenth birthday, when two terrible things happened."

Isabelle caught her breath. Even the marmot stopped digging to listen.

"Firstly, her mother, Mrs. Fortune, died. Mrs. Fortune had been born with a weak heart and one morning, while she was pruning Camoflauge Creepers, her heart stopped beating. Daffodilly rushed home for the funeral and brought a young man with her. His name was Henry, a student who attended Madame Pungent's School for Boys. They were each in their final year of school. She introduced him as her husband, for they had eloped over a long weekend, and she begged Nesbitt to give him a job as a farmhand."

"Was he my father?"

"Yes. He's the second terrible thing that happened, by the way."

Walnut blew his nose again and tucked his handkerchief into his pocket. "When a tender chooses to marry, the spouse must pass a series of loyalty tests before stepping foot on the farm. That's how it must be done. Daffodilly broke the rules and Nesbitt was livid."

"Is that why he's angry?"

"Partially, but there's more." Walnut leaned on the table. "You see, your mother was madly in love and love has a way of making people act, well . . . stupidly. Only those who have been in love can truly understand this. Have you ever been in love?"

"Never," Isabelle replied loudly, to make certain *everyone* in the room could hear her.

"Well, your mother loved your father so much that she entrusted him with many of our secrets. She couldn't imagine that he would ever, or could ever, be disloyal to her family." Walnut shook his head sadly.

Sage brought a pot of tea to the table and handed out three big mugs. His brown eyes caught Isabelle's for a moment. His lips turned up ever so slightly, just enough to say *I'm sorry you have to hear all this.*

"What happened next?" Isabelle asked as Walnut sprinkled sugar into his mug.

"Henry tried to convince your grandfather to start a seed company and to sell the magical seeds all over the world so we'd become the richest family on the planet. But Nesbitt dismissed Henry's idea, of course. Selling magic to the highest bidder is a risky proposition, for what if the highest bidder turns out to be a madman? Or a dimwit?"

Walnut paused to stir his tea. "Henry was relentless in his desire for wealth and one morning he and Nesbitt got into a terrible argument. Daffodilly took her husband's side, telling her father that he was narrow-minded and backward. The next morning, Daffodilly and Henry left the farm and the moment they passed through the tunnel, we knew that Daffodilly had broken her solemn promise as a tender." His eyes welled up with tears again. "Oh, you tell her, Sage."

Sage sat down and folded his hands. "A massive crack appeared in the dome. I wasn't here, that's just what I've been told. The spell was weakened because she took magical seeds off the farm. And the dome has been weak ever since. New holes and cracks appear all the time."

Isabelle felt a rush of shame.

"It is unimaginable for a tender to do such a thing," Walnut said, sniffling. "I knew that love had befuddled Daffodilly's mind but it broke my heart, all the same. And it broke Nesbitt's heart too. Each passing year has driven him deeper into despair until this year when he decided to give it all up. He stopped believing in our future. The world does not deserve magic, he said. We will let the farm die."

The sky had darkened. Stars appeared. Sage lit some candles.

The truth about her parents slowly sank into Isabelle like a skipping stone sinking to the bottom of the sea.

"Where did my parents go?" she asked.

"We don't know all the details but we've deduced that your father took all the magical seeds and abandoned your mother the moment they stepped off the farm. Fortunately, magical seeds are very temperamental, and since Henry did not have the skills to take care of them, most perished. But a few survived and he sold them to the highest bidder, a man with whom you are familiar."

"Mr. Supreme," Isabelle hissed.

"Exactly. Your father celebrated his new wealth by buying the world's largest zeppelin and, befitting his reckless nature, proceeded to crash it into a volcano. He perished."

Isabelle didn't feel too sad about that. Her father sounded like a terrible person. "And my mother?"

"Prepare yourself, my dear," Walnut said. "This is the part I dread telling."

The room fell silent, broken only by Rocky's wheezy breathing. Walnut closed his eyes for a moment, collecting his thoughts, then looked deep into Isabelle's eyes. "Your father told Mr. Supreme all about the Fortunes. And all about Daffodilly, who was homeless and wandering on her own, afraid to return to the farm. Mr. Supreme began to search for her, greedy for the farm's secrets. He almost caught her a few times but she always managed to escape, even though she was heavy with child. Yes, my dear. With you."

Isabelle imagined her mother running from Mr. Supreme,

down dark alleys and muddy lanes. Running and running until she ended up in the place called Runny Cove.

"That's why she left me on the doorstep," Isabelle realized, seeing it all clearly. "She was trying to protect me. She was trying to protect the farm, too. Because Mr. Supreme would have used me to get inside."

"Exactly."

Then came the dreaded question. Isabelle took a deep breath. "Where is she now?"

"I found her body just outside the tunnel. I think she knew that she was dying and wanted to see us one last time, but the spell had turned against her and wouldn't let her back in. It was evident that she had recently given birth, but we didn't know where to find the baby. I buried her in Tender's Cemetery."

"Ten years have passed," Sage said. "But Supreme's gyro-copters still search. I can keep patching the cracks and holes but if one more tender breaks the vow . . ."

Isabelle's mind raced. Sage and Walnut had brought her to the farm, hoping that she could change Nesbitt's mind about letting the farm die. That she, being the last tender, would give him hope. But how . . .

"How did you know where to find me?"

"I knew that a tender, even if she did not know that she was a tender, would influence her environment simply by being alive," Walnut explained. "We sent Rolo out to cover as much territory as possible. He knew immediately when he saw the cloud bogs."

"The cloud bogs?"

 204

"Yes, the wetlands that surround Runny Cove. They are not naturally occurring. The plant growing in them is called Cloud Clover, a highly invasive species that turns dry land into mush. While most plants release oxygen into the air, Cloud Clover releases clouds. You see, the only seeds that survived long enough for Henry to sell were Cloud Clover seeds. In an evil attempt to get more people to buy umbrellas, Mr. Supreme planted Cloud Clover in sunny parts of the world." A sapling shot up from the table where Walnut's hand rested. "Anyone can grow the clover. It germinates and does quite well on its own. But the Cloud Clover growing in Runny Cove is seven times taller than it should be. When Rolo reported this, we knew that a tender had to be living in that horrid village. Rolo continued his investigation and discovered that there were three ten-year-old children. And then Sage delivered the apples, and, well, here you are."

Isabelle's shoulders fell. "I am the reason that it always rains in Runny Cove?"

"It's not entirely your fault. You didn't plant the seed. But you are the reason the cloud coverage is thicker than porridge and why the sun can never break through."

"That's terrible."

No one said anything for a long while. The marmot went back to digging. Isabelle could barely believe it. She was the reason for so much of the misery in Runny Cove. The clouds didn't part because of her!

"What are we going to do about Nesbitt?" Sage asked under his breath.

205

Walnut frowned. "What's that? Did you just call me a twit?"

Sage yanked a mushroom from Walnut's ear. "I said, *Nesbitt*. What are we going to do about Nesbitt?"

"I shall speak to him again. This time I will demand that he allow Isabelle to stay. This time I'll . . ."

"WHY IS SHE STILL HERE?"

Isabelle almost fell off her chair. The booming question ricocheted off the walls and rattled the teapot.

Nesbitt Rhododendrol Fortune stood in the kitchen's entryway, so tall that he had to stoop to fit through. His wrinkled face blazed as furiously as his orange streaks. Isabelle began to tremble.

"I TOLD HER TO GO!"

Chapter Twenty-Four
SAGE'S STORY

Now Nesbitt," Walnut said calmly, "there's no reason for all this shouting."

"I don't want her here. I never wanted her here. Can't you see? She's just like her mother."

Sage stood. "I'm the one who brought her here so if you're going to get mad at someone you should get mad at me."

"I told Sage to bring her," Walnut defended, also rising from his chair. "This was all my idea."

"You both disobeyed my orders?" The question hissed slowly from Nesbitt's mouth, like steam.

Horrible silence filled the room. No one took a breath. Isabelle didn't budge. She could feel her grandfather's stare burn right through her. She wanted to crawl under the table and hide. The marmot, however, found a pebble in the potting soil and threw it right at Nesbitt. *Bonk!*

Stunned, Nesbitt rubbed his forehead.

"I'm s . . . s . . . sorry," Isabelle stuttered. "She likes to throw rocks."

For a moment, the old man's expression softened. Would he change his mind? What could she do to convince him that she wasn't like her mother, that she wasn't going to hurt the farm?

But his eyes narrowed. "The child leaves tomorrow," he ordered. "You will take her back to where you found her. If you don't obey me this time, you can both go with her and never return." He stomped over to the kitchen table. As his hand flew through the air, everyone flinched. But the hand simply landed on the cast iron soup pot. "I'm hungry," he murmured, lifting the pot off the table. As he made his exit, he sneered at the marmot. "And that rodent goes too!"

He stomped down the hall and slammed the door marked "N."

Sage smacked his hand on the table. "Why won't he listen to us?" He kicked a cupboard door. "Why is he so stubborn?"

"Pride, my dear boy," Walnut explained. "He may never recover from Daffodilly's disloyalty."

"But why did he say I was just like her?" Isabelle asked. "He doesn't even know me."

Walnut sat with a weary sigh. "Because, except for the green hair, you are the spitting image of her."

"It's so unfair. We worked so hard." Sage kicked the cupboard again. "All for nothing. For nothing!"

Isabelle's mouth fell open. Is that what she was — nothing?

"Why are you so mad?" she demanded. "You're not the one who has to go back. You don't have to work in a factory or sleep in a rented room, or spend the rest of your life doing dish duty because your landlady called you a thief. You get to stay here and eat hot soup and wear dry clothes. You get to see the sun every day." A panicky feeling flooded Isabelle's body. Like a water bottle filling with seawater, the feeling swirled and bubbled as it moved from her toes all the way up her neck. "You should never have brought me here!" she yelled. She picked up the marmot and ran down the hallway and into her bedroom.

"Isabelle," Sage called.

"Isabelle," Walnut called.

She plopped the marmot onto the bed, then locked the door. She didn't want to talk to Sage or to her great-uncle. She didn't want to see them either, so she locked her window and closed the curtains. Then she threw herself onto the colorful quilt, buried her face into the pillow, and released the tears of a lifetime.

Sometimes a person cries for just one thing — a fall from a bicycle, a failed grade, or perhaps a ruined potato bug palace. But Isabelle cried for so many things that her tears soaked the pillow. She cried for her grandmother and for all the people she missed back in Runny Cove. She cried for the mother she would never know and who had done such a bad thing, and for the grandfather who obviously hated her. She cried because the world was full of mean and rotten people who cared only about making money. She cried because she was the reason for Runny Cove's rain. And she cried for herself and her sorry predicament.

In an instant, Isabelle's dream had been squashed like a bug under Mama Lu's big foot.

"Isabelle?" Sage called softly from the other side of the door. "Isabelle?"

"You lied to me," she said, spitting the words at the door.

"You should have told me that I wasn't welcome here. Go away!" The crying had stuffed up her nose. She stuck her head under the pillow to muffle her sobs. The marmot joined her, puffing warm breath onto Isabelle's cheek.

"We needed to try. We thought that if Nesbitt saw you . . ."

"You lied to me. You said my family was waiting to meet me." She threw the pillow at the door.

"Okay, so I didn't tell you the whole story. If I had told you, you might not have come. I thought I was doing the right thing. Can't you understand?"

"Can't *you* understand? When a girl has never seen the sun she doesn't yearn for it. When a girl has never felt dry she doesn't know what she's missing. But now I know." Every vibrant, colorful, glowing inch of Isabelle *knew* what she had been missing.

Sage tapped on the door. "Isabelle, please let me in. There's something else I didn't tell you."

"Go away! I don't want to hear any more of your lies." She curled into a ball, the way a potato bug does when it wants to protect itself from predators. From *liars!*

The floorboards creaked as Sage slunk away.

Something else he didn't tell me. What else could there possibly be? That she'd be expected to pay for her dinner? That the elephant seal was taking a vacation so she'd have to swim back to Runny Cove? That, come morning, she would be fed to a Piranha Plant?

As night passed, Isabelle lay on her bed like the unhappiest lump of nothing in the entire world. She fell into a fitful sleep. Her dreams churned with angry voices.

You'll have to pay for my apple. Dish duty at my house for a whole month.

She's dead, ya hear me? Dead.

So, little girl, when I tell you that you must work extra hours, I expect gratitude.

There's nothing out there fer ya. Yer just a stupid factory worker.

I DON'T WANT HER HERE!

Isabelle awoke, covered in sweat. She opened the curtains and the window, seeking a cool breeze.

Back in Runny Cove, if Isabelle felt lonely at night and her Grandma Maxine was sleeping, she would look out her fourth-floor window. Even if she couldn't see Gertrude's Boarding House through the rain and fog, it comforted her to know that Gwen slept nearby. But other than the marmot, who sat on her foot, nothing comforted her that night.

"I won't go back," Isabelle whispered. "I won't work for that horrible Mr. Supreme." Besides, who knew what other magical plants might grow if she returned? Maybe one that sucked up oxygen or one that turned rain into ice daggers. She had to run away and she had to do it before the others awoke.

She glanced at the clothes in the closet. That kelp suit would be perfect for her trip, and it wouldn't be stealing because Great-Uncle Walnut had said that everything in the room belonged to her. So she changed into the suit.

"He doesn't want you here, either," she told Rocky. "Looks like it's just the two of us." Rocky seemed to understand, for she stared sadly at Isabelle with her round black eyes. Then she touched her wet nose to Isabelle's freckled one. Together, they climbed out the bedroom window and started across the yard.

Each footstep felt heavier than the last. She didn't dare look back, knowing that she'd start to cry again. She wanted to stay, with all her heart. There, in that fairy tale place, Isabelle knew that she would never run out of things to collect and take care of. She'd never run out of songs either. She'd never run out of *interesting*.

Her intent was to walk straight through the orchard and find the path that led up to the ridge and tunnel, but Rolo flew from the barn and circled her head. "Caw, caw."

"What do you think you're doing?" Sage hurried from the barn, bits of straw hanging from his hair. "Were you trying to leave without me?" He grabbed Isabelle's arm.

"I'm not going back to Runny Cove," she said, yanking away from his grip. "Never. Do you hear me. Never!"

"Shhh. You'll wake Nesbitt. Let's talk inside."

"No."

"If you don't come inside and talk to me, then I'll wake Nesbitt anyway," he threatened.

She didn't want to talk, but she didn't want to wake her grandfather either. She followed Sage to the barn. As he lit a candle, some of the animals awoke. The oxen snorted a greeting. The goats raised their bearded faces.

Isabelle stood in the doorway. If she went inside, he might trap her. "No one can make me go back."

Sage rubbed sleep from his eyes. "You won't survive out there. Not without me."

"You're wrong," she said, scowling. "You think I'm just a stupid factory girl."

Sage folded his arms and shook his head. "I don't think you're stupid, Isabelle. It's just that you don't have the survival skills. I know. I ran away when I was seven. If it hadn't been for Nesbitt, I'd be dead."

The chickens clucked softly, repositioning themselves on their roost. Isabelle took a cautious step inside. "What happened?"

Sage pushed aside a blanket and sat on a pile of straw. Dim candlelight flickered, throwing shadows across his dark face. "I grew up in a port town, way down south," he said. "My parents indentured me to a seaweed soup factory when I was six years old. Do you know what that means, to be indentured?" Isabelle shook her head. "It means that they sold me to the factory's owner. I don't know how much money my parents got for me but that doesn't really matter. What matters is that I knew, even at age six, that I wasn't about to work in that factory for the rest of my life, standing at that conveyor belt every day, pressing labels onto soup tins. So, when I turned seven, I ran away."

Isabelle was too stunned to speak. Sage had been a labeler?

"I figured that the best way to get out of a port town was by boat, so I stole aboard the biggest ship I could find, a Magnificently Supreme Shipping Company ship."

"Really?"

"Yep. I stole food every night from the kitchen and slept down below where they kept the ropes. After thirteen days at sea I overheard some of the crew saying that we'd reach the next port by morning. I knew they'd need the ropes to dock the ship and I didn't want to get caught. I waited for nightfall, then crept up on deck. I could see land and it didn't seem very far away, so I climbed over the railing and jumped into the water."

Sage picked a piece of straw from his hair and rolled it between his long brown fingers. His eyes took on a faraway look. "I made two mistakes that night. I miscalculated the distance and I didn't realize that the water would be so cold. My arms and legs started to feel like stone and the land didn't get any closer. I went under. The next thing I knew I was lying across the back of an elephant seal with a man who introduced himself as Mr. Nesbitt Fortune."

"He saved your life," Isabelle whispered.

"Yep. And he gave me a home. And I've worked hard ever since because I love this place. But you can't imagine how bad it's been with Supreme searching all the time. We can barely leave the farm anymore." Sage flicked the piece of straw.

"I'm sorry about the farm," Isabelle said, pulling the

marmot away from a chicken's nest. "I really am. But I'm not going back to Runny Cove. You of all people should understand why."

"Runny Cove is a rotten place; I know that. But at least you have a home there. You have people to watch over you. That's something."

"But I don't have a home. Grandma Maxine is dead and the room on the fourth floor is destroyed," she said. "And Mr. Supreme will make me work until my fingers fall off. I won't go back and that's final." With Rocky tucked under her arm, she started walking toward the barn door.

"There's still something I haven't told you," Sage said.

"It won't change my mind."

"I think it will."

Isabelle hesitated. She didn't want to know anything more. She didn't want to feel any sadder or any more frightened. But curiosity pushed the word "What?" out of her mouth.

"Your grandmother is not dead."

Chapter Twenty-Five

ESCAPE FROM FORTUNE'S FARM

For the first time in her life Isabelle wanted to hurt another human being — not just dump porridge on his head, or kick him in the shins, or say something mean, but to physically cause pain. Anger shot through her body. She clenched her jaw and fists. How dare Sage say that her grandmother was still alive? Of course he was lying again, trying to trick her so she'd go back to Runny Cove. Then he could tell Nesbitt that he had taken her back, just like Nesbitt wanted. How could he be so cruel?

She was done with him. Done with them all. Enough with the lies and sad stories and fake friendships. She broke into a run.

"Don't run off. Just listen to what I have to say," Sage pleaded.

Isabelle ran across the yard and toward the field that sparkled in the silver moonlight. Though she pumped her legs with all her might, Sage's legs were longer and faster and he didn't have an overfed marmot in his arms. He ran ahead, then turned, blocking her way.

"That day, when you were at the factory, I went to see your grandmother."

"I'm not listening," Isabelle said, weaving around him.

Sage followed, blocking her again. He spoke so quickly she could barely understand. "I knew that if I could get her blessing, it would be easier to convince you to go to the farm with me."

Again, Isabelle tried to scoot past, but this time he reached out and grabbed her around the waist. They tumbled into the tall grass. The marmot whistled as Isabelle struggled to break Sage's grip, but he easily pinned her to the ground. The marmot climbed onto his back and bit his ear. "Ouch," Sage cried, releasing one hand to push the marmot off. But still Isabelle couldn't break free.

"Listen to me," he begged. "You've got to listen. Then I'll let you go."

"I don't want to listen," Isabelle hissed. The marmot scurried around in circles, searching for a rock.

"You don't have a choice! Just sit there and listen to me and then you can run off to wherever it is you're running off to."

"Fine!"

They glared at one another, their faces so close that Isabelle could see the moon in his brown eyes. He released her and she scooted away, hugging her knees. Sage put out his hand, deflecting a perfectly aimed rock. The marmot whistled, then wedged herself between Isabelle's feet.

Sage's expression darkened. "Like I said, I knew that you wouldn't leave Runny Cove without your grandmother's permission, so while you were at the factory, I knocked on Mama Lu's door." He relaxed a bit, his breathing slowing. "Mama Lu opened the door and said, 'Who are ya and what do ya want? I ain't lettin' ya in unless yer the new cheese delivery man or yer the undertaker come to take away that old lazy bag of bones upstairs.'"

Isabelle shivered, for he had mimicked the landlady's voice surprisingly well.

"I didn't have any cheese so I told her that I was the undertaker. 'Well it's about time she died,' Mama Lu said. 'She was a useless, good-fer-nothing invalid, that's what she was. It'll be good to get rid of her.'"

That sounded exactly like something Mama Lu would say. Isabelle clung to every word.

"Mama Lu told me I'd have to go up to the fourth floor to collect the body. I hadn't realized how sick your grandmother was until I saw her. She couldn't even open her eyes. Walnut had packed a Curative Cherry so I could give it to you, Isabelle, but I gave it to your grandmother instead. She seemed so close to dying. It worked immediately. She got right out of bed and gave me a hug. Then she walked around the bedroom and said, 'Isabelle was right. This moss carpet makes my feet feel wonderful.'"

Isabelle gasped. "You're lying," she whispered. "You only know about the moss carpet because you sent Rolo to look in my window. Why are you doing this?"

Sage continued. "I told your grandmother that I knew your real family. That I had been sent to collect you. I told her that you would live on a farm where you could grow all sorts of plants. She was thrilled. 'Will you give her a magical cherry?' she asked. I promised that I would. 'Could she go to school?' I answered yes. 'Would she have to work in a factory?' I told her never. 'How did you get up here?' she asked and I explained that I had pretended to be the undertaker.

"Your grandmother sat quietly for a while, then made a decision. 'Isabelle must go with you. There's nothing for her in this place. She's an intelligent girl. She deserves a better life. But she'll never leave, not as long as I'm alive. She must think that I am dead and that the undertaker came and got me.'

"I didn't argue with her. I knew it would be easier for you to leave if you believed that your grandmother had died. It wasn't the right thing to do, I realize that now, but I was thinking about the farm, Isabelle. You must believe me. I didn't want to hurt you."

Isabelle said nothing. She thought only of Grandma Maxine, standing in moss, feeling better after eating a Curative Cherry. Could it be true?

"Your grandmother and I decided that I would continue to play the part of the undertaker. I carried her downstairs, past Mama Lu, who clapped her hands as if she were watching a parade. Then I carried your grandmother around to the back of the house and through Boris and Bert's basement door. 'I'll hide here,' she told me. 'Take Isabelle away from Runny Cove with my blessing. One day you can tell her how proud I am of her and that I hope she's found the life she deserves. Tell her that I hope she finds her own apple tree.'"

221

Isabelle knew, with that last statement, that Sage was not lying. She hurled herself at him. "I hate you," she screamed, hitting his chest with her fists. "You should have told me that she was alive. I hate you, hate you, HATE YOU!"

He didn't defend himself, but sat rigid as she hit him one last time. Then she staggered to her feet. "Don't follow me. I don't want to see you or this place ever again."

This time she didn't want to look back. This time the farm could burn, for all she cared. She couldn't trust any of them. They were no better than Mr. Supreme, willing to do whatever it took to get what they wanted. Willing to tell her anything to save their precious farm. Willing, even, to break her heart.

Isabelle reached the orchard and stumbled down its path, Rocky following along. The fruit trees rustled as she passed, their leaves whispering, *Tender, tender.* She ignored them, running as fast as she could until she came to the Curative Cherry.

She stopped running. Cherry-covered branches hung high above her head. Nesbitt didn't need those cherries, not as long as he planned on letting the farm die. But she knew people who desperately needed them, people who spent every day of their lives weakened by coughs and congestion. Why should she keep her solemn promise? She owed the Fortunes nothing. But she owed the people of Runny Cove everything because she was the reason why the sun never shined. Nesbitt thought that Isabelle was just like her mother. Maybe she was. But by breaking the solemn promise she wouldn't be helping a greedy businessman. She'd be helping her friends — her true friends.

"Tree," she said. "May I have some of your cherries?"

The tree shuddered, then lowered a branch. Isabelle quickly plucked as many cherries as she could and stuffed them into her kelp suit's pockets. But surely she needed more than what her pockets could hold? A basket sat beneath a nearby tree. She grabbed it and filled it as fast as she could.

"Thank you, tree."

You're welcome, Isabelle the Tender. I wish you success with your quest.

Clutching the basket, Isabelle started up the steep road toward the ridge. She looked back a few times to make certain that Sage wasn't following. She searched the sky and didn't see any sign of Rolo, either. Her legs were already worn out from the climb up the mountain to deliver the spool of thread, but she pressed on. As she walked, the light began to change. Morning was on the way, bringing with it the tendrils of orange and gold that had first greeted her arrival — when she had believed that her future was as bright and shiny as the sun itself.

Upon reaching the top of the ridge, she didn't linger or gaze out at the valley. *I don't want to look,* she thought. *I want to forget.*

She crouched and waited as Rocky climbed onto her shoulder. Then, hugging the basket to her chest, she entered the tunnel. Her eyes hadn't forgotten how to see in dim light but she made her way carefully, catching her boots only a

223

few times on jutting rock. When she came to the end of the tunnel she took a deep breath and held out her hand. One touch would part the Camouflage Creepers and reveal the tunnel's exit. One touch from a tender.

As she hesitated, her palm floating a mere inch from the wall, her old song came to mind:

Beyond the town, beyond the mill
beyond the river, beyond the hill
lies the land of Nowhere
and Nowhere lies there still
for no one goes to Nowhere
and no one ever will.

Nowhere had turned out to be a place called Fortune's Farm, a place protected from the outside world for a good reason. If Isabelle broke her solemn promise by taking the cherries, then the spell would be broken and outsiders would come to Nowhere. Rotten, evil outsiders like Mr. Supreme. He'd steal seeds and plant Cloud Clover everywhere. He'd turn the world into a landscape of rain and umbrella factories. In her desire to help the people of Runny Cove she'd make it possible for Mr. Supreme to hurt countless others. No matter how angry she felt, how betrayed or used, she couldn't do it. She couldn't break the promise.

Though her outside had changed, inside she remained good and true.

Isabelle turned the basket upside down. The cherries fell

224

to the ground, their quiet *plunks* echoing along the cave. She emptied her pockets. She'd have to find another way to help her friends. Somehow, she'd find another way.

She touched the rock wall. It trembled as vines appeared, twisting and fanning until enough space had opened for her to step through.

Clutching Rocky, Isabelle Fortune took a long sad breath and stepped out of Fortune's Farm. The vines settled as the tunnel closed behind her. She shut her eyes and pressed her face into the marmot's warm fur. Worry, doubt, and fear washed over her. What if she couldn't find Neptune? What if she ran into one of Mr. Supreme's gyrocopters? What if . . . ?

"Isabelle."

Isabelle slowly raised her face, fearful of what she would find.

Her grandfather, Nesbitt Rhododendrol Fortune, stood in the clearing. Eve the cat brushed against his leg. He held his arms wide and laughed the deep hearty laugh of a man whose faith had just been restored.

"You've done it, Isabelle. You've passed the test!"

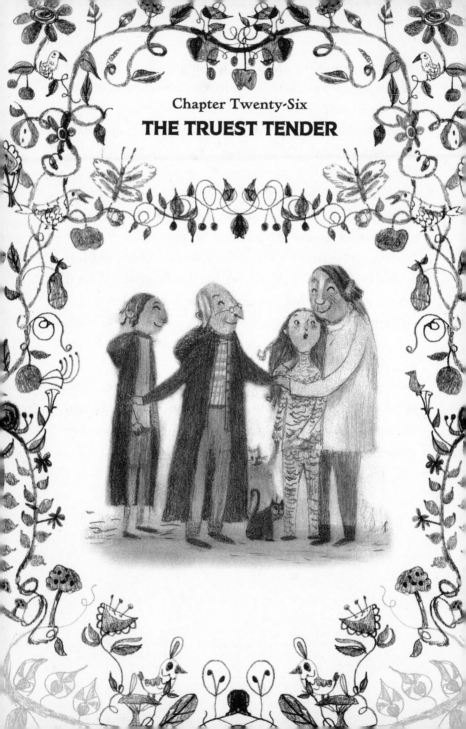

Chapter Twenty-Six
THE TRUEST TENDER

Isabelle thought that a Vice Vine had attacked her, but it turned out to be a hug.

Her grandfather smelled like dirt and grass and fireplace smoke. "Oh, sweet, sweet Isabelle," he said, his voice cracking with emotion. "Please forgive me for putting you through all this, but I had to be certain."

Her face squashed against his cape. The marmot chirped nervously.

"My granddaughter. My beautiful granddaughter." Nesbitt squeezed again, then released his arms.

Isabelle stumbled backwards, taking a deep breath. Was her grandfather crazy? He had yelled at her, had told her to go away. But no anger blazed across his face, no venomous words shot from his mouth. His green eyes twinkled, his wrinkled face crinkled joyfully. "You're a true tender," he said. "The truest of us all. Look at you. Look at your hair. That is the most magnificent hair I've ever seen." Eve purred in agreement.

It wouldn't have been possible for Isabelle to feel more confused than she felt at that moment. Of all the twists and turns her life had taken over the last few days, this was the most puzzling. She strained her neck to look up at Nesbitt's face. Like a tree, he towered over her. "I don't understand," she said.

"I had to test your loyalty, Isabelle. Hold no grudge

against your great-uncle or against Sage. They acted on my orders."

Sage and Walnut stepped out from behind some bushes. Each wore a long, hooded cape. Walnut skipped forward, dancing the same jig he had danced on the bridge when Isabelle's hair had turned green. "She did it, she did it. I knew she would, I knew she would." His wispy hair floated as he twirled around.

"What did I do?" She searched through the kelp suit's pockets, worried that she might have missed a cherry. "I didn't take anything. I promise."

"Exactly," Nesbitt said. He bent down on one knee, bringing his face level with hers. "You had all sorts of reasons to break your promise. But in the end you proved yourself honest. I almost gave up. I fired all the farmhands and stopped working because I thought it was over. But then Sage found you." He spread his arms out like branches. "The future of the world can't lie in just anyone's hands, now can it? Certainly not. But a Fortune with a curious mind and a hero's heart and a head of brilliantly green hair, now that's the kind of person the world can rely upon."

Isabelle's confusion began to clear. "You mean, you like me after all?"

"Like you? We *adore* you," Walnut sang, twirling so hard that he bumped into Sage.

"We love you," Nesbitt said softly.

"You . . . love me?" Only one other person had ever said those words to Isabelle. She took a step back, shaking her head in disbelief, the marmot perched on her shoulder. "You don't think I'm just like my mother?"

Nesbitt's knee creaked as he stood. "You're like your mother in all the ways that your mother was good, and kind, and special. But because you were raised as an outsider, I had to put you through a test," he explained. "Before Sage became the farm's protector, he also had to pass a test. But he proved himself trustworthy, just as you have."

Sage hadn't said anything. He kept his distance, avoiding Isabelle's gaze. Nesbitt leaned over and whispered in Isabelle's ear. "The lies were entirely my doing. Sage does not deserve your anger. He is the truest protector this farm has ever employed."

"Does this mean that you want me to live on the farm?"

"We want that more than anything in the entire world!" Walnut cried.

"And Rocky?"

"Rocky can stay too," Nesbitt said.

"But you seemed so mad," Isabelle said to her grandfather, not quite ready to believe. "You yelled so loudly."

"That, my dear, was acting." Nesbitt bowed as Walnut enthusiastically applauded. "Had I not been born a tender, I'm certain I would have joined the theatre. When I was a schoolboy, I had the lead role in Madame Pungent's production of *Prince Arthur and the Land of Half-witted Trolls.*"

"I played the part of the Land," Walnut called out. "I grew my own costume."

"You're not going to let the farm die?"

"Never," Nesbitt said. "Though I've felt sad for a very

long time, I could never let the farm die. A true tender could never do such a thing."

The farm wouldn't die. She and Rocky could stay. But confusion still clouded the moment. "So what is true? Is my grandmother alive or not?"

Nesbitt patted the marmot's head. "She's very much alive and very well. One of our ravens just returned from checking on her."

A smile burst onto Isabelle's face. "She's alive? She's well? Sage was telling the truth about giving her a cherry?"

"Yes," Nesbitt replied. "It looks like we have a happy ending."

"Happy, happy, happy," Walnut chanted, kicking up his short legs.

Isabelle laughed and all the bad feelings from last night washed away like gray water down the drain. She could barely contain her excitement. She started dancing around like Great-Uncle Walnut. The marmot scampered between their feet, nearly tripping them. Sage leaned against a tree, watching with amusement. A happy ending for a skinny factory worker from the most miserable place on Earth.

"Wait." Isabelle stopped dancing. "It's not a happy ending. What about Runny Cove? What about my grandmother and my friends and the rain and the factory?"

"What *about* your grandmother and your friends and the rain and the factory?" Nesbitt asked, raising his eyebrows.

"I still want to go back. I . . . need to go back."

"Whatever for?" His eyes twinkled in a teasing way.

"I want to give Curative Cherries to everyone in Runny Cove and get rid of all the Cloud Clover so the sun can shine." She waited for his reaction. Only he could give permission to take things from the farm. Would he get angry again? She folded her arms. "I'm going back. Even if you won't let me take some cherries, I still have to try to get rid of the clover. I'll do it by myself, if I must."

Nesbitt, Walnut, and Sage exchanged knowing looks. "I think that giving everyone in Runny Cove a Curative Cherry and digging up all the Cloud Clover is a grand plan," Nesbitt said. "What do you think, Sage? Can we risk another trip to Runny Cove?"

Sage stepped forward; his usually brooding face had softened. "I've covered the caravan in Camouflage Creepers so it can't be seen by gyrocopter." He lifted some vines to reveal the oxen. "And I loaded the cherries into the back just as you ordered."

"You ordered?" Isabelle asked.

"Sage told me about your plan," her grandfather said. "He also told me that he wanted to help you. So I gave him permission to collect some cherries." Sage, Walnut, and Nesbitt threw off their capes. Each wore a bright green kelp suit.

Even though he tried to escape before she reached him, and even though he looked about as unhappy as a barnacle without a shell, Isabelle gave Sage a great big Vice Vine hug.

"Well, what are we waiting for?" Walnut asked. "Let's go."

Farewell, Isabelle, the trees whispered. *Safe journey to you.*

"Goodbye," she replied, waving to the swaying pines.

Nesbitt looked around. "Who are you waving at?"

"The trees," she explained. "They have whispery voices, don't you think? They sound kind of like the wind."

"I wouldn't know," Nesbitt said, smiling and stroking his chin. "No one's had the power to hear the trees since the first tender. Dear, dear Isabelle, what a surprise you've turned out to be."

Nesbitt gave Eve the cat instructions to watch over the farm. She rubbed against his leg again, then she pranced through the tunnel, her tail held high and proud. The vines closed behind her.

As Nesbitt and Walnut climbed into the camouflaged caravan, Isabelle smiled at Sage. He actually smiled back.

"It's going to be a happy ending," she whispered.

Long before they reached the beach, Isabelle knew that Neptune had arrived because it smelled as if she had stuck a fish up each of her nostrils. At the shore's edge, Sage unhitched the oxen. "They will take care of themselves until we return," he told Isabelle as the mighty creatures wandered back to the forest.

"GREETINGS, KING NEPTUNE," Nesbitt yelled, bowing to the seal. "IT IS AN HONOR TO BE IN THE COMPANY OF YOU AND YOUR IMPOSING NOZZLE. WE HUMBLY REQUEST YOUR SERVICES AGAIN."

Sage and Walnut removed the caravan's wheels, then

pushed the caravan into the shallows. Neptune and two of his wives arranged themselves as Sage attached ropes around their middles. Then Sage jumped onto the driver's bench, ropes in hand, with Rolo on his shoulder.

Walnut pulled a jar from his kelp suit pocket. "These are Ocean Motion Olives," he told Isabelle, dropping one into her hand. The little sphere undulated. "It mimics the ocean's movement inside your stomach so your stomach doesn't become confused by the motion outside."

"Tenders are people of the land, so sea travel usually disagrees with us," Nesbitt added, eating an olive. Recalling the dizziness and upchucking, Isabelle eagerly ate hers.

Walnut pulled his knit hat over his bald spot and climbed into the caravan. "I'd better get my beauty sleep. Might meet myself a single lady or two in Runny Cove." He pulled some moss from his nose, then curled up in the corner.

"Ocean Motion olives tend to make one sleepy," Nesbitt explained, helping Isabelle into the caravan. "You'll find yourself dozing in no time at all."

He spoke the truth. Isabelle's eyelids drooped. Exhausted from her night of bad dreams and her plans of running away, she curled into a corner and drifted to sleep.

"NEPTUNE! AWAY!" Sage cried. And off they went.

Evening's first stars popped into the sky as the caravan reached the Tangled Islands. The marmot woke the sleepy travelers with a robust string of chirps. She pressed her nose against the caravan's window.

Isabelle stretched her arms, then slid next to Rocky.

"That's her island. Sage said that because marmots reproduce so fast, they'll probably run out of food."

Nesbitt yawned, then peered out the window too. "It does look like a small place."

As the island neared, Rocky trembled with excitement, wiggling her stubby tail. Was she remembering her promise?

"Could we help them too?" Isabelle asked. "Could we take them someplace where there's lots of food?"

"I'm not sure where that would be. Let's ask my brother. He knows more about rodents than I do." A few of the olives from Walnut's jar had spilled into his pocket and had sprouted into young trees. Nesbitt pulled the branches aside, looking for his brother. "Walnut, wake up. What do marmots eat?"

"What about my feet?" Walnut asked, sitting up and wiping a speck of drool from his chin. "Do they stink again?"

Nesbitt pulled an olive leaf from Walnut's ear. "Eat, not feet. What do marmots like to eat?"

"Yellow-bellied *Marmoticus Terriblus* or flat-bottomed *Marmoticus Faticus*?"

Isabelle held Rocky in the air, exposing her yellow belly.

"Oh, that kind. Well, the *Marmoticus Terriblus* is a vegetarian by nature, preferring nuts and leafy greens. Their favorite food, however, is clover. A marmot will travel miles for a sweet patch of clover. One marmot can eat three times its body weight in clover in a single day."

Nesbitt turned to Isabelle. "Are you thinking what I'm thinking?"

"Cloud Clover!" Isabelle cried.

234

Chapter Twenty-Seven

CHERRIES FOR
EVERYONE

Saving an entire town is no easy task. A person who sets out to *save an entire town* will probably be judged, by future historians, as having lacked common sense or as being downright loony. But Isabelle had traveled across the ocean and back, had grown green hair, and had spoken to trees. She had almost been killed by a ship, had escaped would-be kidnappers, and had passed a test of loyalty. She wasn't about to let little things like common sense or sanity stand in her way.

But first they stopped at the Island of Mysterious Holes, where Isabelle explained her quest to save Runny Cove. One mention of the abundant Cloud Clover and the marmots raced across the muddy beach and piled into the caravan. Isabelle counted fifty-three, but they wiggled around so much, she could have been off by four or five. After tracking mud everywhere, the critters dug holes in the pillows, cavorted beneath the table, and threw olives at each other. Fortunately, Sage had locked the Curative Cherries inside a small rodent-proof chest. Rocky, after tiring of nose-kissing, joined in the digging.

"I never knew marmots were so rowdy," Nesbitt said as a baby marmot burrowed in his sock. "I think I'll go sit on the driver's bench with Sage."

"He's not fond of rodents," Walnut added after Nesbitt had left.

The night passed slowly and since Walnut seemed to prefer sleep to conversation, Isabelle had lots of time to think. Despite being told so many times that she was just a stupid factory worker, that she was nothing special, that she was unwanted, Isabelle had always listened to the little voice inside. For it is often a little voice that speaks with more wisdom than a big booming voice. And so she thought about all that had happened, and what better place to think than beneath a blanket of sleeping, wheezing marmots?

"Runny Cove!" Sage hollered.

The seals slowed and Walnut opened the door. Gray seeped into the caravan like plague seeps into its victims. Isabelle inhaled a lungful of despair. The marmots huddled fearfully, only their noses wiggling. Nesbitt poked his head inside, rain dripping off his hair. "We're here."

Walnut picked up the cherry-filled chest and stepped out into the shallow water. Rain soaked through his knit hat. "How terrible," he whispered. "I feel so sad. I think I might start crying."

"I swore I'd never come back," Sage said, jumping from the driver's bench. "I must be crazy."

Isabelle waded to the lifeless shore. The rain beat its familiar rhythm on her head. Nesbitt and Sage unhitched the seals and pulled the caravan onto the beach where the marmots disembarked. The Camouflage Creepers worked their magic, blending the caravan into the wet driftwood. Rocky followed the other marmots as they scurried off into the fog.

"Rocky?"

"Don't worry. They can smell the clover," Walnut explained, wrinkling his nose. "But I don't see how with that stench in the air." He pointed to the distant hill where the factory sat, a multicolored plume snaking from its chimney.

"THANK YOU, KING NEPTUNE," Nesbitt said, bowing to the seal. "WE WOULD BE FOREVER GRATEFUL IF YOU AND YOUR PROMINENT PROBOSCIS WOULD AWAIT OUR RETURN." Neptune nodded and rolled onto his back for a belly scratch. "And thank you, lovely ladies," Nesbitt said to the wives, who had perfect hearing. "May I add that both of your rumps are looking plumper than usual." They batted their lashes at him.

The wind stung Isabelle's face and her lower jaw began to tremble. Sadness swooped down and covered her like a blanket. *Can I do this, or have I made a terrible mistake?* she wondered. For sadness can make a person feel small.

Her grandfather, sensing her doubts, placed his hand on her shoulder. His strong, steady grip eased her fear. She wasn't alone. She had two tenders, a protector, and an army of rowdy rodents on her side. The happy ending was at hand.

Sadness only makes you feel small if you let it.

"Follow me," she said.

As dawn's faint rays filtered through the ceiling of clouds, Isabelle led her companions across the driftwood forest, up and over the sand dunes to the edge of the gravel road, midway between the village and the factory.

"How do you wish to proceed?" Nesbitt asked.

"Me?" Isabelle strained her neck to look into his eyes. "You're the Head Tender. Shouldn't you make that decision?"

"My dear Isabelle." His back creaked as he bent close to her. "You have chosen to use magic for its very best purpose — to improve the lives of your fellow human beings. And you made that choice, not after years of study and training, but simply by using your heart. Today, you are the honorary Head Tender."

"Congratulations," Sage said.

"Wow. Thank you." Isabelle's mind raced. What should she do next? "We can't deliver the cherries to the boardinghouses because the landladies will take the fruit for themselves. Believe me. They take everything."

"I like a woman who knows what she wants."

Nesbitt folded his arms. "We are not here to find you a wife, Walnut. Go on, Isabelle."

"We can't take the cherries to the factory because we don't want Mr. Supreme to know about them. Or to know about us."

"Right," Sage agreed.

BAROOO!

Walnut almost dropped the chest. "What was that? It sounded like a dragon's fart. Are there dragons around here?"

"That was the factory's horn," Isabelle explained. "It's time for the workers to leave the boardinghouses." Then it dawned on her. "Almost everyone works at the factory. We can hand out the cherries right here in the road, before they

239

reach the factory. Then Mr. Supreme and his assistants won't see us."

"That seems an excellent plan," Nesbitt said.

And so they waited. The sound of coughing was the first thing to emerge from the fog bank — lots and lots of coughing. Next came the sound of marching feet. Isabelle's feet began to march in place, entirely of their own volition, matching the marching rhythm of the workers. The morning march was as much a part of her feet as her toes and toenails. Then pasty faces and yellow slickers emerged. Row after row of workers walked up the road, with eyes half-closed and faces void of expression, their puckered skin as translucent as the fog. Isabelle brushed her fingers over her smooth, sun-kissed face. No wonder Sage had called her ugly.

"Sadness," Nesbitt said quietly. "They are shrouded in sadness."

As the front of the crowd drew closer, Isabelle stepped into the middle of the road. "Hello," she called out, waving. "I've come back."

One might think that the sight of the four strangers in kelp suits would have stopped the factory workers dead in their tracks. One might think that they would have noticed a skinny boy with tangled black hair, a short old man with long white hair, a tall old man with orange-streaked hair, and a girl with hair as green as a blade of grass. But they continued their steady march up the road, sloshing through the potholes and mud.

"Wait," Isabelle cried.

240

"We can't wait," a worker said. "If we wait then we'll be late."

"But it's me, Isabelle. I've come back. I'm here to help you."

Walnut pulled his glasses from his pocket and slid them onto his wet nose. Then he nudged Isabelle. "Who is that woman with the gray hair and prune-like face?" Of course, he had just described every woman in the crowd. "The one pushing her way to the front? Look how strong she is, how forceful, like a plow. Is she married? I like a woman with spunk."

"Let me through!" Grandma Maxine elbowed her way out of the crowd. Her long braid fell free as she pushed off her slicker's hood and held out her arms. "Isabelle! I heard your voice. Look at you. You're the most beautiful sight I've ever seen."

The very worst part of the last few days was laid to rest as Isabelle hugged her living, breathing grandmother. Grandma Maxine squeezed so hard she lifted Isabelle right off her feet. She had grown so strong, she could probably beat Mama Lu in a game of tug-o-war.

After wiping away tears of happiness, Isabelle took her grandmother's hand. "Grandma, look who I've brought. This is my grandfather, Nesbitt Rhododendrol Fortune."

"It is an honor to meet you," Nesbitt said with a bow. Even when bowing, he still towered over most everyone. "Thank you for taking care of Isabelle. I will be forever in your debt."

Grandma Maxine's smile fell. "Yes, you will," she replied

241

sternly, shaking a finger. "Terrible thing to leave a baby on a doorstep. What kind of people are you?"

"They are good people, really they are," Isabelle said. "This is my Great-Uncle Walnuticus Bartholomew Fortune."

"Please call me Walnut, madame." He also bowed. Even when bowing, he was still squatter than most everyone. "I can't help but notice that you are not wearing a wedding ring, dear lady. Are you, by any chance, looking for a husband?" He smiled eagerly, his drenched hat clinging to his round head.

"Looking for a husband? Why?" Grandma Maxine asked. "Did I lose one?"

"A sense of humor, too." Walnut clapped his hands as if he had just opened a birthday present.

"And this is Sage," Isabelle said. "Oh, that's right. You two have already met."

"You look well," Sage said.

But Grandma Maxine scowled at him. "You promised to take her away. Why did you bring her back? There's nothing for her here."

"It was my idea to come back," Isabelle said. "I want to help. We've all come to help."

"Help?" Grandma Maxine shook her head. "Runny Cove is lost, Isabelle. The best thing you can do is to save yourself."

BAROOO!

Grandma Maxine looked nervously up the road. "That's the five-minute warning. I'll get in trouble if I'm late."

"But Grandma, we brought cherries to cure everyone."

She gasped. "You mean like the cherry I ate?"

"Yes." Isabelle opened the chest. Raindrops glided down glossy cherry skins. "Will you help me pass them out?"

"That's why you came back? To help everyone feel better?"

"And to see you."

Grandma Maxine pulled Isabelle into another rib-cracking hug. "You're an angel, Isabelle. Of course I'll help you pass them out. That nasty Mr. Supreme can give me quadruple shifts for being late — I don't care. I'm going to help my granddaughter!"

The last of the workers marched past. Isabelle held out a cherry to one of the women. "Eat this," she insisted. "It will make your cough go away."

"I don't have time," the woman said hoarsely. "I won't get paid if I'm late."

Walnut, Nesbitt, Sage, and Grandma Maxine tried to convince workers to stop and eat a cherry, but not a single worker accepted the offer. Their eyes focused on one thing only — the factory that loomed at the top of the gravel road.

Isabelle wound frantically up the road, searching for someone who would trust her. Finally, she spotted Gwen. There was no time for a reunion. No time for explanations. "Eat one of these."

"Isabelle?" Gwen mumbled, wiping her runny nose. She barely opened her eyes. "I'm so tired. You're in trouble for missing so much work."

"Please eat this, Gwen. It will make you feel better."

"I don't have time. I have to work triple shifts today," she said, slopping through a pothole. She kept marching, just like the others.

"Leonard," Isabelle called out, running to her friend. But he didn't even recognize her voice.

"Got . . . to . . . get . . . to . . . work."

"They won't listen to me," Isabelle said frantically. "They only care about getting to work."

Walnut put an arm around Isabelle's shoulders. "Don't despair. I'm sure there's a way to get them to pay attention."

"Maybe we can try again tonight, when they leave the factory," Sage suggested.

"But then they'll be in a bigger hurry to get home to their suppers," Grandma Maxine said.

"They won't pay attention, not as long as that factory sits up there," Isabelle cried. "I hate that stupid factory. I wish it would just disappear!"

"That can be arranged." Walnut pulled a seed packet from his jacket pocket and smiled mischievously.

Chapter Twenty-Eight

MARMOTS TO
THE RESCUE

The instant the seeds fell into Walnut's palm, they sprouted. "Seems to me that they can't be late if there's no work to be late for," he said, green shoots flowing down his arm.

"Camouflage Creeper seeds. Great idea," Sage said.

"Hmmm." Nesbitt stroked his pointy chin. "It certainly would be a tasty bit of revenge if we made Mr. Supreme's factory disappear."

Isabelle smiled, imagining Mr. Supreme driving up in his big black roadster to find his factory missing. He'd holler, no doubt about it. He'd throw a fit, but all the while his factory would be right where he had left it. Wouldn't that be a fun sight to see? Even better than the time Mama Lu had hollered all morning about her missing salt canister, and it turned out she'd been sitting on it the entire time!

"You're talking crazy," Grandma Maxine said. "In the first place, no one can make an entire factory disappear and in the second place, what would the workers do? We need that factory to survive. It's the only way for us to earn a living."

"Oh no, Grandma. There are other ways. Believe me."

While traveling across the sea, Isabelle and her companions had devised a plan for how the workers of Runny Cove could earn a living without the umbrella factory. Though using Camouflage Creepers hadn't been part of the original plan, it occurred to Isabelle that everything would be easier if the factory disappeared.

"Let's do it," she said.

"Rolo," Walnut called. The raven flew from the clouds, scooped the Camoflauge Creepers into his beak, then flew toward the factory.

Mr. Hench stood in the factory's doorway. "Hey!" he shouted through cupped hands. The workers had only marched two-thirds of the way up the road. "Get up here, you lazy lot of losers!"

Rolo dive-bombed Mr. Hench's head, then flew around the factory dropping the wriggling creepers. The effect was immediate. The vines took root in the soggy ground and climbed the cement building, grabbing hold of windowsills and fissures. Sprouting branches and leaves, the vines climbed and covered until no doors, windows, or pipes could be seen. Up they rose, reaching the roof, forcing their way down the chimney and extinguishing its stinky plume. In only a few moments the towering cement fortress had been transformed into a solitary mountain. Or so it appeared.

The workers stopped in their tracks. They stared. They shook their heads. They rubbed their eyes. Rain pelted their disbelieving faces.

"Hey. Get a move on." Mr. Hench hadn't yet noticed the mountain. He hurried down the road carrying one of the new umbrellas — azure blue with white polka dots. "Whatcha all standing around for? Get up there and get to work or Mr. Supreme will fire the whole lot of ya."

But the workers just kept staring.

Isabelle, who stood with Sage and her family at the end of the crowd, had not yet been noticed by Mr. Hench. "It worked," she whispered.

"These old eyes have never seen anything like it," Grandma Maxine whispered back.

Mr. Hench poked a few workers with his umbrella. "Move it. Move it, I say. Lazy bunch of good-for-nothings."

"But . . . but . . . but . . ." Gwen stammered. "The factory is gone."

"Where'd it go?" Leonard asked.

Mr. Hench nearly fell over. "What?" He hurried back up the road. "What's going on here?" He poked the mountain with his umbrella. "Where'd this come from?"

As Mr. Hench poked and cursed, the workers of the former Magnificently Supreme Umbrella Factory gave Isabelle their full attention while she explained the wonders of the Curative Cherries. And she thought it best to do so in a little song.

The Fruit Song

Is your phlegm weighing you down?
Does your fever make you frown?
Is the frog in your throat hopping around?
Eat some fruit, eat some fruit, eat some fruit.

Are your boogers cramping your style?
Are your lips too chapped to smile?

 248

Are the sores on your tongue terribly vile?
Eat some fruit, eat some fruit, eat some fruit.

Stop wheezing and sneezing and listen to me,
for I have something that's totally free.
If you're feeling sick it will sure do the trick
but don't eat the stem and spit out the pit . . .

Are you tired of wiping your snot?
Does your breath always smell like rot?
This is better than pills and won't hurt like a shot,
eat some fruit, eat some fruit, eat some fruit.

As Nesbitt, Walnut, Sage, and Grandma Maxine helped hand out the Curative Cherries, they all sang, "Eat some fruit, eat some fruit, eat some fruit."

Isabelle dove straight for Gwen.

"Mmmm, that's good." Gwen's eyes began to sparkle. The crust around her nostrils disappeared. "I feel great," she said. "Isabelle? Is that really you? What happened to your hair? Why did you leave without saying goodbye? Where have you been? I've missed you so much. Mama Lu's been spreading horrible lies about you. She called you a thief."

"I don't care about Mama Lu." Which, for the first time in Isabelle's life, was the truth. She didn't care if Mama Lu took away another privilege, or yelled at her, or called her a stupid dimwit. Mama Lu was as insignificant as a grain of salt. "Could you help Grandma and me pass these out?" She poured some cherries into Gwen's hand. "Find Leonard and give him one. He can help us, too."

Isabelle found Boris and Bert, the Limewigs, and the Wormbottoms. They straightened their backs and legs and held their heads higher than they had ever held them before. "I can breathe," Mrs. Limewig said.

"My headache's gone," Boris said.

"My nose is clear," Mr. Wormbottom said.

Mr. Hench stumbled down the road, waving his umbrella. "I don't know what all the singing's about but we've got a real problem here, people. The factory is gone!"

"I don't see why that's a problem," Grandma Maxine said. "I say, good riddance."

"Look, old woman," Mr. Hench growled. "You don't seem to understand. Mr. Supreme is coming here this morning for an inspection and when he sees that his factory's gone, well, I'm going to be in a heap of trouble."

That comment frightened the workers and they huddled. "He'll blame us," they said.

"No, he won't blame you," Isabelle told them. "I won't let him. I'll tell him that this was my idea."

"That's too dangerous," Sage said. "I'm the protector. I'll tell him that it was my idea."

"I'm not afraid of him any longer," Isabelle said. Which, for the first time in Isabelle's life, was the truth.

And at that very moment, it stopped raining. A patch of blue appeared directly above the gravel road.

"The marmots have made a dent in the Cloud Clover," Walnut said.

The blue patch widened, pushing away the clouds. Workers turned their faces toward the sky. Yellow rays trickled down, caressing their heads and drying their slickers. Grandma Maxine held up her arms. "It's the sun," she said. "The sun has returned."

Some who stood on that road could remember the days when Runny Cove had been a sunny, happy place. But for the young ones, like Gwen and Leonard, the glowing sky was a sight they had never dreamed possible. As the villagers cast off their slickers, the gray that had soaked into their bodies began to evaporate. Mold patches dried up. Hair turned blond, brunette, red, and black. Irises ignited. Gwen took Isabelle's hand, her blond curls bouncing. "It's the sun, Isabelle. I'm so glad we get to see it together."

Leonard wandered up, his birthmark less noticeable on skin that had turned brown. "Isn't this great?" he asked. "It's like a dream."

"Let's go to the beach," Boris said to Bert. "We haven't made a sandcastle since we were kids."

"Let's take a stroll," Mr. Limewig said to Mrs. Limewig. "Remember how strolling used to be our favorite thing to do?"

"Let's do absolutely nothing," Mrs. Wormbottom said to Mr. Wormbottom. "I can't remember the last time we did absolutely nothing."

Gwen and Leonard somersaulted down the sand dunes

while Leonard's parents waltzed off down the road. Even Mr. Hench got caught up in the happiness, announcing that he was going to dig for buried treasure. Soon everyone had wandered away, holding hands, laughing, running, and leaping. Grandma Maxine, Isabelle, Sage, Nesbitt, and Walnut watched with quiet satisfaction.

"Isabelle, you should be very proud of yourself," Nesbitt said. "You've brought a bit of happiness to Runny Cove."

"I couldn't have done it without all of you. Without . . . my family."

BEEP! BEEP!

Isabelle's heart lurched, then somersaulted. "Oh no. Here comes Mr. Supreme." It's easy not to feel afraid of someone when that person is far, far away. But now she wasn't so sure.

A black roadster barreled up the road. Walnut whipped out his packet of Camoflauge Creepers but not soon enough — they had been spotted. The driver slammed on the brakes, skidding to a stop just inches from Nesbitt. The driver's door opened and Mr. Supreme slid out, his shiny black coat crunching as he stood. "What have we here?" His intense gaze swept over Isabelle, then the others, coming to rest upon Walnut's seed packet. "I presume that I have the pleasure of finally meeting the Fortunes?"

Walnut shook his head, trying to hide the seeds, but Nesbitt stepped forward. "Your presumption is correct." Though Nesbitt's voice remained calm, his hands clenched angrily behind his back.

Mr. Supreme slid a pair of sunglasses onto his nose and unbuttoned his driving coat. "I see that you've brought your magic with you. What have you done with my rain?"

"The Cloud Clover was not yours to plant," Nesbitt said.

"Those seeds were stolen property," Sage added, bravely stepping forward. Isabelle's heart pounded faster. Mr. Supreme still terrified her. *I'm not as brave as I thought.*

"Stolen property?" Mr. Supreme's upper lip glistened. He pulled a canister of antibacterial wipes from his pocket and dabbed his lip. "I had no idea. The man who sold them to me said nothing about *stealing* them."

"Where else have you planted the clover?" Nesbitt asked.

Mr. Supreme raised his pencil-thin eyebrows. "I'm sure I don't know what you're talking about." He didn't even try to make it sound like the truth. He delighted in his lies. Isabelle wanted to punch him right in the nose.

Mr. Supreme ran his gloved hand along the roadster's chrome. "I'm willing to make a deal, Fortune. I suppose you'd like me to stop searching the Northern Shore with my gyrocopters. That could be arranged but only if you bring my rain back."

Nesbitt took a long, deep breath. *Is he considering the proposition?* Isabelle wondered. Calling off the search would make life less worrisome at the farm and would make Sage's job a lot easier, but at a terrible cost.

A little smile sat on Mr. Supreme's face. He might have excelled at ruining people's lives, but he stunk at lying.

"Don't believe him." Isabelle stumbled forward, grabbing her grandfather's arm. "He'll keep looking. I know he will."

"And who are you, little girl?" Mr. Supreme glared over the rims of his sunglasses.

Isabelle remembered how scared she had felt that morning in the factory, when she had told him that she couldn't work more hours. She remembered her trembling hands, the way her words had squeaked out of her mouth, the way everyone had watched as she, a stupid factory worker, had tried to appeal to Mr. Supreme's sympathies. This time it would be different. She put her hands on her hips. "I'm the one who got away," she said proudly.

"What?"

"You tried to catch my mother and me but we both got away."

"Isabelle," Nesbitt hissed. "Say no more."

"I want him to know," she insisted. "I want him to know that he can't make everyone do what he wants."

"Can't I?" Mr. Supreme narrowed his eyes. "I do believe I'm looking at a young tender. How very interesting." He removed his driving gloves and twirled them as he leaned against the roadster. "Perhaps you would like to come and live with me, little girl. I can offer you a much better life. A palace, a gyrocopter of your own, riches beyond your imagination. What could these old men possibly offer you?"

Isabelle took a deep breath, ready to launch into a long list of things.

"Isabelle," Sage warned.

She had taken the oath. No one had to remind her of that. But oh, how she wanted to tell Mr. Supreme that all his riches could never compare to one square inch of Fortune's Farm.

"Just tell me what you want and I'll make it happen," Mr. Supreme said.

"I want *you* to go away and never come back to Runny Cove."

He snorted. "I have no intention of going away. Share your magic with me and you'll be the most famous little girl in the entire world."

"But you see, I have shared my magic with you." Isabelle pointed up the hill. Sage, Walnut, Nesbitt, and Grandma Maxine stepped aside.

Mr. Supreme's smiled faded. "What have you done?" he cried, staring at the mountain. A flock of seagulls nested on its peak. He whipped around and glared at Isabelle. "What have you done with my factory?" He lunged at her.

Grandma Maxine wrapped her arms around Isabelle while Sage, Nesbitt, and Walnut stepped in front of her, providing a protective wall that Mr. Supreme would have to fight his way through.

"Your factory is gone," Nesbitt said. "The rain is gone. There's nothing for you in this town."

"We want you to go away!" Isabelle cried.

Mr. Supreme shook a fist. "I made this town. These people can't survive without my factory. They need me."

"Do they?" Nesbitt asked. "They don't look like they

255

need you." He pointed to the sand dunes where the Limewigs happily strolled. Some kids were playing catch with a factory hard hat and Mr. Hench was digging in the dirt with his umbrella handle.

"Hench?" Mr. Supreme shouted. "HENCH! WHAT ARE YOU DOING?"

Mr. Hench glanced up and smiled. "I'm collecting potato bugs."

Mr. Supreme whipped off his sunglasses. "Potato bugs?" He stomped to the road's edge. "I don't pay you to collect potato bugs. Get back to work, all of you. GET BACK TO WORK!"

But no one paid him any mind. They just kept strolling, and playing, and digging.

Mr. Supreme cursed. But then a fake smile spread across his face and he steadied his voice. "Come now, Fortune. Surely we are men of reason."

"You are lucky that I am a man of reason," Nesbitt said between clenched teeth. "For there's many a man who would kill you for what you did to my family."

"That's all in the past," Mr. Supreme said. "But the future is bright. With your magic and my wealth, we could rule the world."

Rage flashed across Nesbitt's face. "Your kind have ruled the world for far too long." He straightened to his full height, casting a shadow across Mr. Supreme. "Isabelle spoke true. It's time for you to go away."

Mr. Supreme snickered. "I'm not afraid of you."

Uncle Walnut cleared his throat and reached into one of his pockets, pulling out a seed packet. "You seem to be a fan of our seeds," he said, waving the packet in the air. "Perhaps you would like to try these?" He ripped the packet with his teeth and poured a single seed into his hand. It sprouted, then started to grow.

Mr. Supreme raised his eyebrows eagerly. "Changed your mind about making a deal? What is it?"

"Piranha planticus," Walnut said. "A carnivorous plant that prefers living flesh." The plant sprouted a fish-like head with enormous fangs. Walnut held it at arm's length. The fangs eagerly gnashed the air. "It seems rather hungry, wouldn't you agree?"

Mr. Supreme backed up, his gaze darting wildly between the plant and Nesbitt's looming frame. "What's to keep me from coming back tomorrow? Or the next day, or the next?"

Isabelle knew what would keep him from coming back — the only thing that mattered to him. She squirmed free of her grandmother's arms and marched right up to Mr. Supreme, holding her chin as high as she could. "If you ever come back to Runny Cove, I'll travel all over the world and make every one of your factories disappear!"

"And I'll go with her," Sage said.

A rock soared through the air and hit Mr. Supreme's car. Then another rock and another. The marmots appeared at the edge of the road. They raised themselves onto their back legs and took aim.

"Hey, stop doing that," Mr. Supreme cried as rocks rained down. "Watch the paint job. It's fresh out of the factory!"

A rock hit Mr. Supreme in the head and Isabelle knew, without even looking, which marmot had thrown it. "Good girl," she whispered.

The Piranha Plant growled furiously and grabbed Mr. Supreme's coat, tearing off one of the sleeves. Rolo swooped and pecked Mr. Supreme on the nose. The plant grabbed the other sleeve and more rocks flew, but Mr. Supreme escaped by jumping into the roadster's driver's seat. As the engine burst to life, he rolled down his window. "I have your word, Fortune, that if I don't return to Runny Cove, you'll leave my other factories alone?"

Nesbitt nodded.

"So be it. But mark my words, you tenders haven't seen the last of me."

Then he sped away, leaving behind a nasty-smelling black cloud and a whole bunch of happy people.

Chapter Twenty-Nine
SUNNY COVE

Rolo flew high above an orchard where trees stood in tidy rows, their branches weighed down by red, orange, and purple fruit. Usually when he scouted the orchard, Rolo saw dozens of people climbing ladders and filling baskets. But on this day, except for the occasional scurrying marmot or darting blue jay, the orchard lay still. Rolo caught an undercurrent and lazily circled over the trees he had helped to plant. One by one, he and Great-Uncle Walnut had deposited squirming seeds into land that had once been suffocated by Cloud Clover.

Rolo pumped his wings and picked up speed, following the gravel road to the factory. Out front a huge painted sign read: SUNNY COVE JUICE COMPANY. Usually the factory buzzed with activity but on this day it sat quiet. Rolo passed over a chimney that had once spewed stinky smoke. A nest of sticks perched on top. The nest's owner, a great blue heron, paid her respects as Rolo flew by.

A breeze, carrying the scent of salt and waves, caressed Rolo's wings. He dipped lower, his shadow gliding across the sand dunes and the driftwood forest. In the distance, sunlight danced upon clear water. Under Sage's guidance, Neptune and his wives had pulled the rotting fishing boats from the cove. Isabelle and her friends had planted oyster and clam seeds. Slowly but steadily the fish had made their return. From the corner of his black eye, Rolo caught their silver shapes as they darted between beds of kelp. A gull screeched at him, worried he might steal its clam. But something else had caught his attention.

All along the speckled beach people stood holding brightly colored umbrellas, some with tassels, some with rhinestones and stripes. The people were brightly colored as well, wearing their Sunday best on a Friday afternoon. Rolo scanned the crowd until he saw the boy with the tangled black hair. He lowered his wings and gently landed on the boy's shoulder.

"Hello, Rolo. How'd the scouting go?" Sage asked.

Rolo nodded his head.

Sage walked to the front of the crowd, where the girl with green hair stood. She smiled at Sage. She and her friend Gwen wore matching dresses and held bouquets of flowers, as did Mrs. Wormbottom and Mrs. Limewig.

Then the girl with the green hair, whom Rolo had come to know and love, began to sing.

The Sunny Cove Song

I never thought that life could feel
warm and dry and bright.
I never knew that things could smell
sweet and clean and light.
But now I know and it's clear to me,
that Sunny Cove is the place to be.

Sunshine shining down,
songbirds flying 'round,
seedlings in the ground,
happiness to be found,
here in Sunny Cove.

Walnut fumbled through his pockets, pulling out packets of seeds, handkerchiefs, and wads of paper. "I can't find it," he mumbled. "I've lost it. What am I going to do? I've lost it."

Nesbitt cleared his throat and handed a golden ring to his brother. "You haven't lost it. You asked me to hold it."

Walnut clapped his hands. "Oh, what a relief. Thank you." Then he slipped the ring onto Maxine's finger. "With this ring, I thee wed," he said.

A cheer erupted amongst the villagers. Walnut almost fell over from all the slaps on his back. Grandma Maxine gave Isabelle a hug and kiss. She waved as she and Walnut climbed into the caravan. "Have a nice honeymoon," everyone yelled. Boris, Bert, and Leonard pushed the caravan into deeper water. Two of Neptune's wives pulled it to the sea.

"We'll leave soon," Sage told the bird.

Rolo nodded again, then took flight. There was one last place he wanted to check.

He flew to the village, over streets that no longer stood underwater, over rooftops that no longer leaked. He flew past a sign that read: BORIS AND BERT'S BED AND BREAKFAST, and another that read SUNNY COVE ELEMENTARY SCHOOL. He followed the street called Boggy Lane until he came to its end.

While everyone else had been pleased with the changes in Sunny Cove, one particular group of residents had not — the slugs, which had lost most of their damp places to live. Sage thought it only fitting that one should be provided. So he and Rolo had secretly planted a single clump of Cloud Clover behind the house that stood at the end of Boggy Lane. Above that house, and above that house alone, a permanent cloud hung, dark and fat with endless rain. And so the village slugs had packed their bags and had moved into Mama Lu's Boardinghouse.

Rolo landed on a windowsill and folded his wings. He pressed his eye to the foggy glass. The observation chair rocked from side to side as a large woman in a blue bathrobe shook an empty salt canister in the air. "SLUUUUG!" she hollered. "Gertie, get me some salt!"

Another woman stood on the kitchen table. The floor glistened with gooey, happy gastropods. "I keep telling you that there ain't no salt in the market. They don't allow it no more."

"SLUUUG! SLUUUUUUUUUUUUUUUUUUUU-UUUUUG!"

Rolo chuckled, for even a raven is blessed with a sense of humor.

He took to the sky once again, speedily making his way past the cove and out to sea. He spotted the seals as they swam powerfully across the water. Nesbitt rode in front, on one of Neptune's wives. Isabelle and Sage sat in Neptune's saddle, sea wind blowing through their hair and across their smiling faces as they made their way back to a place that wasn't supposed to exist. Rolo thought about joining them but decided to fly for a while longer.

The day was just so nice.

For another fun-filled adventure
from Suzanne Selfors, don't miss
SMELLS LIKE DOG.

Meet Homer Pudding, an ordinary farm boy who's got big dreams to follow in the footsteps of his famous treasure-hunting uncle. But when Uncle Drake disappears, Homer inherits two things: a lazy, droopy dog with no sense of smell, and a mystery. Join Homer and his friends on an adventure as they discover that treasure might be closer than they ever imagined....

TURN THE PAGE FOR A SNEAK PEEK!

AVAILABLE NOW

1

Breakfast
with the Puddings

What Homer Pudding didn't know on that breezy Sunday morning, as he carried a pail of fresh goat milk across the yard, was that his life was about to change.

In a big way.

What he did know was this: That the country sky was its usual eggshell blue, that the air was its usual spring-time fresh, and that his chores were their usual boring, boring, boring.

For how exciting can it be cleaning up after goats?

And that's what Homer had done for most of his twelve years. Each year his chore list grew longer, taking more time away from the thing that he'd rather do. The one thing. The only thing. But it was not playing football, or riding a bike. Not swimming, or fishing, or building a fort.

If he didn't have to rake goat poop, or change straw bedding, or chase goats out of the flower bed, Homer Winslow Pudding would have more time to dream about the day when he'd become a famous treasure hunter like his uncle.

"Daydreaming doesn't have any place on a farm," his father often told him. "There's too much work to be done."

But Homer dreamed anyway.

Mrs. Pudding waved from the kitchen window. She needed the milk for her morning coffee. Homer picked up his pace, his rubber boots kicking up fallen cherry blossoms. As he stumbled across a gnarled root, a white wave splashed over the side of the bucket. Warm goat milk ran down his sleeve and dribbled onto the grass where it was quickly lapped up by the farm's border collies.

"Careful there," Mr. Pudding called as he strode up the driveway, gravel crunching beneath his heavy work boots. He tucked the Sunday newspaper under his arm.

"Your mother will be right disappointed if she don't get her milk."

Homer almost fell over, his legs tangled in a mass of licking dogs. "Go on," he said. The dogs obeyed. The big one, named Max, scratched at a flea that was doing morning calisthenics on his neck. Max was a working dog, like the others, trained to herd the Puddings' goats. He even worked on Sundays while city dogs slept in or went on picnics. Every day is a workday on a farm.

And that's where this story begins—on the Pudding Goat Farm. A prettier place you'd be hard pressed to find. If you perched at the top of one of the cherry trees you'd see a big barn that sagged in the middle as if a giant had sat on it, a little farmhouse built from river rocks, and an old red truck. Look farther and you'd see an endless tapestry of rolling hills, each painted a different hue of spring green. "Heaven on earth," Mrs. Pudding often said. Homer didn't agree. Surely in heaven there wouldn't be so many things to fix and clean and haul.

The dogs stayed outside while Mr. Pudding and Homer slipped off their boots and went into the kitchen. Because the Pudding family always ate breakfast together at the kitchen table, it was the perfect place to share news and ask questions like, *Whatcha gonna do at school today?* or *Who's gonna take a bath tonight?* or *Why is that dead squirrel lying on the table?*

"Because I'm gonna stuff it."

"Gwendolyn Maybel Pudding. How many times have I told you not to put dead things on the kitchen table?" Mr. Pudding asked as he hung his cap on a hook.

"I don't know," Gwendolyn grumbled, tossing her long brown hair.

Homer set the milk pail on the counter, then washed his hands at the sink. His little brother, who everybody called Squeak, but whose legal name was Pip, tugged at Homer's pant leg. "Hi, Homer."

Homer looked down at the wide-eyed, freckled face. "Hi, Squeak," he said, patting his brother's head. Squeak may have been too young to understand Homer's dreams, but he was always happy to listen to stories about sunken pirate ships or lost civilizations.

"Get that squirrel off the table," Mr. Pudding said, also washing his hands at the sink.

Gwendolyn picked up the squirrel by its tail. The stiff body swung back and forth like the arm of a silent metronome. "I don't see why it's such a problem."

"It's dead, that's why it's a problem. I eat on that table so I don't want dead things lying on it."

Confrontations between Gwendolyn and Mr. Pudding had become a daily event in the Pudding household, ever since last summer when Gwendolyn had turned fifteen and had gotten all moody. In the same breath she might laugh, then burst into tears, then sink into a brooding silence. She befuddled Homer. But most girls befuddled Homer.

He took his usual seat at the end of the pine plank table, hoping that the argument wouldn't last too long. He wanted to finish his chores so he could get back to reading his new map. It had arrived yesterday in a cardboard tube from the Map of the Month Club, a Christmas gift from Uncle Drake. Homer had stayed up late studying the map, but as every clever treasure hunter knows, a map can be read a thousand times and still hide secrets. He'd studied an Incan temple map eighty-two times before discovering the hidden passage below the temple's well. "Excellent job," his uncle Drake had said. "I would never have found that at your age. You're a natural born treasure hunter."

But the new map would have to wait because the morning argument was just gathering steam. Clutching the squirrel, Gwendolyn peered over the table's edge. It wasn't that she was short. It was just that she almost always sat slumped real low in her chair, like a melted person, and all anyone saw during meals was the top of her head. "You eat dead things all the time and you eat them on this table so I don't see the difference." She glared at her father.

"Now Gwendolyn, if you're going to talk back to

your father, please wait until we've finished eating," Mrs. Pudding said. She stood at the stove stirring the porridge. "Let's try to have breakfast without so much commotion, like a normal family."

"And without dead squirrels," Mr. Pudding added, taking his seat at the head of the table. "Or dead frogs, or dead mice, or dead anything."

"But I've got to practice. If I don't learn how to make dead animals look like they ain't dead, then how will I get a job as a Royal Taxidermist at the Museum of Natural History?"

"Gwendolyn said *ain't*," Squeak said, climbing next to Homer. "That's bad."

Mr. Pudding shook his head—a slow kind of shake that was heavy with worry. "Royal Taxidermist for the Museum of Natural History. What kind of job is that? Way off in The City, with all that noise and pollution. With all that crime and vagrancy. That's no place for a Pudding."

"Uncle Drake moved to The City," Gwendolyn said, emphasizing her point with a dramatic sweep of the squirrel. "And he's doing right fine."

"How do you know?" Mr. Pudding asked with a scowl. "We don't even know where he lives in The City. All he's given us is a post office box for an address. And we haven't heard a word from him since his last visit. Not a letter. Not a postcard. What makes you think he's doing right fine?"

"No news is good news," Mrs. Pudding said. She set bowls of porridge in front of Mr. Pudding and Squeak, then set a bowl for Gwendolyn. "Now stop arguing, you two, and eat your breakfast. And put away that squirrel."

Gwendolyn stomped her foot, then tucked the squirrel under her chair.

As Mr. Pudding stirred his porridge, steam rose from the bowl and danced beneath his chin. "I told him not to go. The City's no place for a Pudding. That's what I told him. But he said he had *important matters* to tend to. Said he had to find out about that pirate, Stinky somebody or other."

"Rumpold Smeller," Homer corrected, suddenly interested in the conversation. "Duke Rumpold Smeller of Estonia became a very famous pirate. His treasure has never been found. Uncle Drake wants to be the first person to find it."

Mr. Pudding groaned. Gwendolyn rolled her eyes.

"Eat your porridge, Homer," Mrs. Pudding said, setting an overflowing bowl in front of him. Then she planted a smooch on the top of his curly-haired head.

Mr. Pudding motioned to his wife. Though she bent close to him and though he whispered in her ear, everyone at the table could hear. "Why'd you give him so much? Don't you think he's getting kind of…*chunky*?"

She put her hands on her hips. "He's a growing boy. He needs to eat." Then she smiled sweetly at Homer.

Now, Mrs. Pudding loved all three of her children equally, like any good mother. But love can be expressed in different ways. For instance, Mrs. Pudding knew that her eldest child had a mind of her own, so she gave Gwendolyn lots of room to be an individual. Mrs. Pudding knew that her youngest child wanted to be helpful, so she gave Squeak lots of encouragement and praise. And Mrs. Pudding knew, and it broke her heart to know, that her middle child was friendless, so she gave Homer extra helpings of food and more kisses than anyone else in the house.

"Growing boy," Mr. Pudding grumbled. "How's he ever gonna fit in if he can't run as fast as the other boys? If all he talks about is treasure hunting? It's my brother's fault, filling his head with all that nonsense."

It's not nonsense, Homer thought, shoveling porridge into his mouth. So what if he didn't fit in with the other boys? All they cared about was fighting and getting into trouble. He pulled the bowl closer. And so what if he was chunky? A true treasure hunter would never pass up the chance to eat a warm breakfast. Near starvation while stranded on a deserted island had forced more than a few treasure hunters to eat their own toes.

"I like twesure," Squeak said, porridge dribbling down his chin.

"I like treasure, too," Homer said.

Mr. Pudding drummed his calloused fingers on the table. "Could we go just one meal without talking about finding treasure? Or stuffing dead animals? I don't know where I went wrong with you children."

Mrs. Pudding poured herself a cup of coffee, then added a ladle of fresh milk. "There's nothing wrong with having *interests*."

"*Interests?*" Mr. Pudding scratched the back of his weathered neck. "Stuffing dead animals and finding lost treasure—what kind of interests are those? Why can't they be interested in goat farming? Is that too much to ask? Who's gonna run this farm when I'm too old to run it?"

"Me," Squeak said. "I like goats."

As sweet as that sounded, it gave Mr. Pudding no peace of mind. Squeak was only five years old. Yesterday he had wanted to be a dragon-slayer.

"Goat farming's honest, solid work," Mr. Pudding said, dumping brown sugar on his porridge. "You children don't understand the importance of honest, solid work."

Gwendolyn rolled her eyes again. Then she sank deeper, until her bottom was hanging off the edge of her chair. Homer was bored by the conversation again. He tried to dig a hole in his porridge but the sides kept caving in—like trying to dig for treasure in mud.

Now, Mr. Pudding loved all three of his children equally, like any good father. But he didn't believe that giving them extra room to be individuals, or giving extra encouragement or extra food and kisses, did much good. Solid work meant a solid life, which in turn meant a roof, and a bed, and food on the table. What could be more important than that?

Mr. Pudding pushed his empty bowl aside, then unrolled the Sunday *City Paper*. "Wouldn't surprise me one bit if I started reading and found out that my brother had been robbed or had fallen into a manhole. I'm sure something terrible's gonna happen to him. The City's a terrible place."

As he read, muttering and shaking his head, the children finished their breakfast. Gwendolyn carried her bowl to the sink, as did Homer.

"Mom, when I'm done cleaning the stalls, can I go read my new map?" Homer asked.

"Of course." Mrs. Pudding kissed Homer's soft cheek, then whispered in his ear. "I believe in you, Homer. I know you'll find treasure one day."

Homer looked into his mother's brown eyes with their

big flecks of gold—like coins half-buried in the sand. When he became a famous treasure hunter, he'd give all the jewels to her so she could wear a different necklace every day and buy new dresses and shoes. And one of those fancy crowns that beauty queens wear.

But chores came first. He started for the kitchen door when Mr. Pudding waved the newspaper and hollered, "I knew it! I knew something terrible would happen to him!"

Ready for more excitement?
More magic?
More FUN?
Collect all the adventures by Suzanne Selfors!

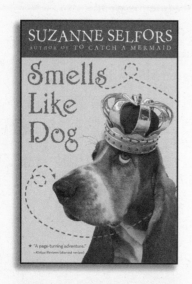

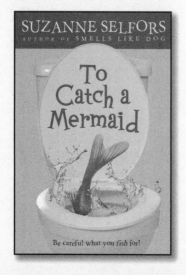

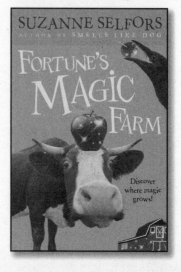